Sarah Elliot was born in Newcastle and raised in Northumberland. She was diagnosed with dyslexia at the age of ten and turned to writing her own stories as a way of keeping up her skills. She has never looked back since.

She graduated from Swansea University in 2009 with a Masters in Creative and Media Writing and has had three plays performed by a theatrical group in Swansea. She currently works as an administrator in a care home in Newcastle and spends her free time socialising with friends, writing and taking Petal the Rottweiler for long walks.

A Simple Wish

Sarah Elliot

A Simple Wish

To Luca

Hope you enjoy

S. Elliot

Vanguard Press

VANGUARD PAPERBACK

© Copyright 2014
Sarah Elliot

ISBN 978 1 84386 959 7

Vanguard Press is an imprint of
Pegasus Elliot MacKenzie Publishers Ltd.
www.pegasuspublishers.com

First published in 2014

Vanguard Press
Sheraton House Castle Park
Cambridge England

Printed and bound in Great Britain

To my parents, Lynn and Kevin, for always giving me support, friendship, and love.

Part I – The Sister I Never Had – John misses his mother dearly after a car crash claimed her life five years ago and one night makes a wish on a shooting star to see what life would be like if she was still alive. Much to his surprise, the wish is granted and he gets to spend one more day with her. But his biggest surprise comes in the form of Phoebe, his twin sister of whom he knew nothing about.

Part II – The Brother I Never Had – Two years later, Phoebe prepares to go to a Halloween ball with her new boyfriend but still feels that there is something missing from her life. When the opportunity for her to grant a wish occurs, she wishes to see her twin again and John comes back into her life for one more day.

Part I

The Sister I Never Had

Chapter 1

Sunshine

The braying of Amberly and Diesel as they chased madly around after Alan, clearly enjoying the clement weather, caused a smile to creep slowly across John's face. It was the first smile of the entire day for the blond-haired boy and it didn't go un-remarked. "Ha, the cloud has finally been lifted, I knew it wouldn't take you long." The cheeky grin was oh so typical of Scott but for once the older brother used it to lighten the situation rather than prove a point that he had won.

Not that there was really anything to win between the two eldest brothers, they had had their fair share of successes over the years and had planned their lives out to a certain extent so many years before that now everything was a long waiting game. They had never been rivals at school or for affection from their father due to a four year age gap so they had invented a sort of friendly 'better than you' game in order to have something to keep them going.

"Oh shut up," John replied, leaning his chin down onto his hands with half a sigh, "it's hard not to smile when those three get going."

Scott chuckled, watching the two Springer spaniels chasing after the swimming-trunk-clad six-year-old who was their youngest sibling. The boy looked almost a carbon copy of John, with his blond hair but had his father's green eyes. They were a deep emerald green, captivating and filled with mischief, though hopefully one day that would change to some form of wisdom. Though Scott really didn't want to think what the tiny terror would be by the time seven years had rolled by. "Heh, I know what you mean." He clapped John on his shirt clad back and grinned. "Makes me wish that I was still able to do such a thing."

Looking up to the tanned and well worked out body which almost glistened in the sunshine, John scowled at the other, "The only reason you're not doing so today is cause you're not sure if Penny's going to turn up and you don't want to ruin your six-pack with sand." It was always the same argument and normally spoken in good jest but today the boy just didn't feel like joining in the fun of the seaside.

He was not like his older brother who was at the virtual peek of physical perfection nor was he like his half-crazy younger brother who could easily get away with running around with Amberly and Diesel cause it looked cute. John was spindly, drawn out almost as if his body couldn't quite decide what to do with itself and no matter how hard he tried he could never get a bronzed looking tan. If he was left out in the sun without being covered for more than five minutes he tended to end up looking like a tomato and it wasn't fun in the slightest.

Sometimes he envied his brothers; they had definitely gotten the lion's share when it came to looks. Even Vincent, the middle brother who was swanning off in some distant part of the world in order to play his wonderfully composed music, whilst dressing like a suicidal duck still managed to out rank him in the looks department. John felt that he had been deliberately swapped with someone else, just in order for there to be a contrast between the family members.

The only thing he could truly say that he even remotely liked about himself was his eyes. They were a light shimmering blue, like sunshine bouncing off the waves that lapped in. They dazzled many a person and were unique in the family of five men because they belonged to his mother.

Sighing, Scott ruffled the young man's hair and shook his head, "I know, kiddo, but there are just some things that you have to let go sometimes. I bet you Mum is going to be fuming because you're not having a good time, on her birthday as well."

Elbowing the other in the stomach, none too gently, John tried to change subjects, think of anything but that horrific night five years ago and move on with the rest of the day. The only problem of course was the fact that this whole day revolved around his mother and celebrating her life. It had become the traditional thing to do, since doing anything on the day she had died always proved to be far too emotional for all involved so this was the best compromise that they had come up with. To celebrate the day that Lucy Henderson had come into the world and enjoy the happy memories that brought them all.

But for some unknown reason, this particular year her second son was just not in the mood to do so. If he had the choice he would have gladly stayed in bed, under the blankets and wept openly for many long hours but sought no comfort. Scott backed off slightly, recognising the signs that the other wanted to be left alone but not prepared to do so today. For a while his eyes followed the black, white and brown speckled dogs as they fought back and forth over a large stick which then snapped in two causing both to go running off in completely different directions.

Their father, Jeff, a tall ex-military man with a greying crew-cut, set off yelling loudly after the dogs despite not knowing which one to chase off after first. Alan, having grown bored, started attempting to finish digging a hole to the very centre of the earth which was his current fancy. The boy looked so determined in his task that Scott was thankful they had a caravan to go back to, because the very thought of being stuck in a three hour long car journey with a very tired six-year-old was something that he did not want to comprehend.

Tilting his head back towards John, he was only mildly surprised to see the once only blond male had slumped further forward so that his eyes were resting on his knees. Despite the fact that the younger had put on the longest pair of swimming trunks, sensible shoes, a white vest top and a light blue shirt, it was clear to see the red lines forming along the skin. It was more than probable that he wouldn't sleep tonight if they weren't treated and Scott knew that the sooner it was done the quicker things would return to normal.

"Come on, Spocky," he said, pulling himself up and rather ungraciously scooping the younger male into his arms, "someone needs a good wash down."

Receiving next to no complaint from the other, which in itself was quite a feat and a half, the journey back to the caravan was undertaken without any hassle. It wasn't until they were back inside and Scott had laid the other down did he realise why. The back of John's neck was red raw and the burns had started to creep around the front. "Oh, you old girl," he commented dryly, running his fingers through the soft blonde hair, "you're never going to get anyone like that now are you?"

John looked up sheepishly, his eyes large and unsure of the situation but holding an apology. Rolling his eyes, Scott once again ruffled the hair and went to close the curtains but found John's hand latching desperately onto his arm. "I dreamed… last night," the voice was raw, like the jagged edge of a tin can.

Placing a light kiss on the fifteen-year-old's forehead the dark haired Henderson smiled lightly, "I know, I was there. Just rest quiet here for a few seconds, okay?"

Over the years Scott had gotten used to dealing with this situation when it cropped up. Ever since the other was born he had suffered from albinism though unlike a majority of cases it was harder to see. Granted his mother had been aware of the trait running in the family for some time and had taken steps to ensure that the chances were reduced, but John still had the genetic coding which could cause problems. Thankfully the doctors had been able to do something in order to help out as well but since Scott was no medical student, and never liable to be, he had just accepted the fact that his brother sometimes needed extra care and attention.

Having closed all the curtains and blinds, the dark haired man made his way quickly over to the bathroom and turned on the taps. The water couldn't be freezing cold nor scorching hot, it had to just be a sort of lukewarm that took years upon years of practice to achieve. At one time he had been absolutely rubbish at getting it right, now it was one of the art forms which he cherished dearly. Satisfied with the water temperature and level, the nineteen-year-old returned to his brother to gently remove the clothes he wore before placing him in the water.

If it had been anyone else, Scott would have been all fingers and thumbs over the whole situation but this was a perfectly normal situation to them. One that had been played out a thousand times over and would probably be played out a thousand times again. "On the count of three," Scott joked as he plopped John into the water, smiling at the slightly strained chuckle which escaped from the other. "Now I've only brought Mr Duck-Duck with me, will that be okay for, sir?"

John glared at his brother. "You're annoying." A cough followed but he couldn't help but appreciate all that Scott did for him, he really was wonderful indeed. In one way he didn't want the other to go off to university in the next few months, it just wouldn't feel quite the same. Not that the older man would have answered any questions on such a subject right now since he was busy cleaning away as much of the dead skin as he could from his very pale brother, and once again wondering about the curious shaped scar on John's left hand side.

It was long, like someone had cut into the skin in numerous different places but kept it flowing from one central spot. There was no real explanation for it, though he had asked his father more times than he could count, but had never received an answer which satisfied his curiosity.

"Scott?" John asked at length, trying to distract the other from the scar which often had him worrying about what had really occurred in his early life and get him to talk once again as he felt more inclined to do so now.

Shaking his head to snap himself out of his thoughts, Scott looked up at John. "Sorry, what do you want?"

John considered his answer for a few seconds. "What would Mum think of us all?"

Chapter 2

Wishing

For a long while, Scott was quiet, tending to John's abrasions and fetching the cream which they always had to order in especially. It wasn't that he didn't want to answer that particular question, especially on a day like today, it was just that he couldn't quite think as to how would be the best way. He knew in his heart what he thought of them all but substituting that for someone who meant so much to them was not going to be a nice thing to do to anyone. Tactfully he busied himself, trying to gain time by doing things that required concentration and careful application. It was his way of saying 'give me time to think' without offending anyone. Though there were plenty out there who just presumed that he had no opinion on the matter and would pass it off as a stubborn refusal to speak.

Not five minutes later, John was lying on the sofa with his back exposed to Scott's careful hands as he rubbed the sticky cream into the pale skin. For a second he thought of bringing up the topic again but opted against it, he knew better than to push for something that wasn't going to come willingly. Scott, getting the impression that he had to speak at least a few words to break up the silence between them, finally began to tackle the problematic question in the only way he knew how. "I'm not sure what she would think, to be honest." It was always remarked in his school reports that he wasn't exactly the most flowing of people when it came to the English language. "I can only hazard a guess at everything but you know Mum, she was always full of surprises."

John blinked his eyes, staring at nothing in particular and trying to piece together the vital pieces of information that Scott was not saying. He was a great believer in the unspoken word but right now his brain was filled with far too many variables due to the stinging sunburn. At least the cream was helping to get rid of the sting but it would be a long while before it was completely gone. "I do know one thing though," Scott cut into his thoughts with another cheeky grin, "she would be over the moon that a certain someone has been offered a scholarship."

"I don't even know if I'll get the grades to fully take up that scholarship as of yet, Scott." John's face looked even redder now that he was blushing. "It's not guaranteed in the slightest."

Rolling his eyes skyward, the elder couldn't help but begin to draw a smiley face on the others back with the cream, "You have been the smartest out of all of us ever since you started watching *Countdown* when you should have been watching *Thunderbirds*."

"I did watch that show," John immediately shot in though still utterly failing to hide the blush, "it was one of my favourites. Dad should have known better than to change channel half way through."

"But that's the whole point," Scott replied, whilst the large friendly hands worked on obliterating the smiley face, "most kids would have just walked away in sheer boredom but you grabbed hold of a sheet of card, a red crayon and started working it all out on your own. Love your brains, John; they're far better than any of ours."

Before the young man who couldn't stand the light that often could reply, Jeff returned with Alan and the two dogs. Debates about things that happened in the past which could affect the future were quickly lost in the tirades of food, getting Alan to bed and trying to stop Diesel licking all the vital cream off of John's back. Bedlam wasn't the correct word to describe the situation but it came pretty close to it on a few occasions. Finally the darkness of night drew in and the curtains could be opened a little so that the stars were visible.

Jeff sent Scott off to bed around ten thirty, telling him to call his pretty lady friend and confirm that all was going according to plan for the garden party she was having. Once he was gone, the ex-military father smiled as he sat down next to John and lovingly helped him onto his back so that his head could rest upon the left leg. It was something that father and son had always done though John never knew quite why. When he was younger odd thoughts had occurred to him that someone else should be on his father's right hand side at the same time that he was lying or sitting like he did. There was no real reasoning behind it, just a hidden knowledge that something – or more correctly someone – was missing from that knee.

Only once had he attempted to lie on the opposite side when getting comforted but found that it was one of the worst experiences of his life. It was like someone was there who wasn't happy about him taking their place and he had worked himself up into such a fettle that he swore never to do so again. Jeff had never dared comment on it past that one incident though the look in his eyes said that he possibly knew something more. John however did not wish to find out anything more about the incident and it just passed away as a mere odd occurrence that had happened one night.

"Feeling better?" Jeff asked his son at length, gently running his hand through the blond hair and trying not to pull too much of it out. Scott had somehow managed to learn a trick to keeping all the hair on top of the other's head but unfortunately for the father he had a habit of taking a fair amount out without meaning too.

John gave a tight smile before nodding silently and sighing. The burns had gone down a little and were just constantly humming with a slight bit of pain. "I guess you're going to sleep here tonight, right?" Jeff always hated one sided conversations, they brought back memories of fights he had with Lucy and how she could always win anything by just being silent. "Do you need anything at all?"

John started to shake his head but then paused and licked his lips. "No, Scott... care." Clearly the pain was getting to his second son as his speech patterns were a little off.

"Hey don't wreck yourself on my behalf," Jeff said with a knowing smile. "I don't want to have to send you back to the hospital again."

Another scowl crossed the young man's face and Jeff couldn't help but chuckle lightly at the youth below him. "Okay, no more hospitals. I promised remember. I'm going to put a movie on because I won't fall asleep for a while, want to help me pick one?"

Nodding, John lay staring at the ceiling for a few long moments whilst his father went to choose the movie. Quietly he reflected on their good fortune at being able to afford so many luxuries but didn't dwell too hard. Picking the film, John settled down to watch with his father, glad to be receiving this sort of comfort tonight. Normally it would drive him crazy but right now it was graciously received.

Strangely though, John found he could barely focus on the screen despite the film being one of his favourites. He wasn't even really aware that the dogs had come in and were slouched across his feet, nor that Jeff was snoring lightly above him. It felt like the world was almost at a standstill, yet still moving gently as if he were on some form of lazy river ride in a water park. His eyes weren't dropping and no yawns escaped him, there was just the screen which shone a lively blue white colour. After a while, though, he could have sworn he imagined it, a sphere of white light – not blinding but soft and gentle – appeared to slowly creep out of the screen. Like a child meeting someone for the first time.

Blinking at the sphere caused it to change into a young girl, possibly no older than four or five. She had deep olive-coloured skin, long flowing golden hair and a white free flowing dress which pooled around her. Though John barely noticed any of these small facts at it was the girl's completely white eyes which caught his own blue ones and made them shimmer gently. "You have been chosen John Henderson, to accept a gift that few ever receive. Though it shall only be temporary." The voice sounded old, full of wisdom and prowess but at the same time was innocent, childlike and playful. It reminded John of the first snow drops in spring, the little white flowers which would push their way through the snow and almost appear to say 'spring is returning'.

"I have?" he asked stupidly, still captivated by all that was going on and having no real clue as to what he was supposed to do in this situation.

The child nodded. "Speak but one wish and it shall be granted to you."

John had heard of these sorts of stories before, he had read so many books on the subject and knew that he had to be careful. It was a bit childish to take this all for real but right now the teenager was prepared to give anything a go. He knew what he would wish for if he were given half the chance, had known for the last five years what it would be and now here was a young girl offering him the chance to have the wish.

"I wish to see what life would be like if my mother were still alive," he said carefully but found his attention drawn towards the slumbering Jeff's right knee. There was still nothing there, like always, but something told him that there was this time.

The girl smiled before bowing low, "Before the clock strikes, your wish shall be granted. Sleep now and awake with new light."

Panic gripped briefly at John's heart as the girl suddenly glowed brightly, filling up the entire space for only a moment before disappearing with a snap. Blinking rapidly to clear the spots which were dancing about in front of his eyes, John stared around the living room of the caravan. It was exactly the same as before, the film however was long over and only static was showing. For a moment he considered going up and turning the set off but then his eyes felt heavy and sleep took him.

Not before, just very faintly, almost on the verge of hearing he heard the words, "Wish granted." The clock ticked around and chimed out the hour.

Chapter 3

Granda Micha

"Hey, Spocky," Scott's voice drifted into the hazy pre-awoken mind of John after about five minutes of trying, "time to wake up before all the food's gone."

With a groan, John blinked open his eyes glad to find that the curtains were still drawn closed which was a good thing. Yawning loudly, the lanky teenager turned to glance at his older brother who was smiling once again but there was a knowing glint in his eyes. "What?" the younger asked, drawing out the syllables to emphasize his full question.

Only to find himself suddenly being pounced upon by Alan who let out an all mighty yell of, "I got the heffalump!" that mixed in with Scott's laughter to the point where it was very hard to hear anything else. Managing to roll off the sofa, John grabbed his youngest brother and tackled him to the ground. Doing so was a feat upon itself as trying to convince the young rascal to calm down was akin to putting out a fire with a cup of water but for reasons that he couldn't quite figure out, John was in a playful mood this morning which was probably a good thing.

"I am not a heffalump, you wriggly octopus!" he said, rolling back and forth across the floor. "You ain't got no right to call me such things."

Alan just laughed, flailing his arms about as he was hoisted off the ground. "I can and I will! 'Cause you are the biggest Heffalump in the whole wide world!"

Before John could reply there was a sudden upsurge of a bark and Diesel decided to make a leaping appearance. Consequently the Springer landed fully on John's stomach, knocking the wind out of him but being still only five months old the dog barely noticed and kept on running around like a mad thing. Thankfully Scott stopped having one of his bigger laughter fits and caught the collar before the black headed dog could do any more potential damage. "Come here, you ragamuffin! You can't be going around doing crazy things like that. Let's go find your sister before you break John anymore today." Wrestling the hyperactive dog away, Scott winked at the two blond brothers. "Don't spend too long down there, breakfast will be gone and eaten before you know if it you're not careful."

"Granda wouldn't do that!" Alan said, scampering away to find the kitchen. "Granda cooks the best in the world!"

Sitting up slowly, John frowned only slightly at the thought that their grandfather was cooking anything but brushed it off as being one of those days. Maybe his father had been called away by work once again and instead of cutting the holiday short, he had asked Granda Micha to watch the boys for an hour or two. The only way to get any form of explanation was of course to get up off the floor and go and find out but for some odd reason the blue eyed boy didn't feel like doing so as of yet. It wasn't that the smell of bacon and eggs wasn't appealing, his stomach was growling louder than it normally did but there was just something off with the whole situation.

There was nothing visibly wrong, everything was exactly where it had been the night before and the DVD he had been watching had been returned to the shelf as it ought to have been but something in the back of his mind was nagging him that things weren't right. Glancing down at himself, he confirmed the sunburn from yesterday and reasoned that was probably the source of his unease. He hated being sunburnt because it usually meant he couldn't go outside and enjoy some time with his family but at least he had a couple of good books to actually start reading. Brushing his worries aside as it appeared that he had found the answer to his problem; John got up and headed to the kitchen to see Granda Micha waving a spatula at Alan.

"If you so much as take another piece of bacon to feed to them dogs I swear that I'll take you upon my knee and smack your little behind until it's redder than a baboon's bottom," the thick Jamaican accent clipped along perfectly with the man's outward appearance, "now go and play outside and keep out of my hair as my old Hannah would say. Go on, be off with you."

Granda Micha was Lucy's father and a very lively character indeed. He always appeared to be in the process of cooking, cleaning, fixing something up, and chasing wild dingoes despite the fact that there were none anywhere about, or just doing something to keep his mind occupied and his body healthy. His dark skin and black hair shimmered with years upon years of hard graft and work whilst his dazzling blue eyes pierced through almost to your very soul when he was mad. Though this was a rare thing as Granda Micha was probably one of the biggest teddy bears on the planet with a rumbling laugh that was infectious. He didn't like seeing people hurt or upset and was always the one to turn to when things went bad.

Some of John's school friends had been highly surprised to discover his Jamaican Grandfather but the story was easily explained. Grandma Hannah had been a volunteer teacher out in Jamaica in the early fifties when she met Micha at a local dance. Of course at the time there had been a whole scandal about a 'white' woman going off with a 'black' man but Hanna had bravely turned around to anyone who said anything and said, "Small minded people will never understand the true feeling of being in love," before walking off without so much as a glance backwards. John had always been proud of his Jamaican family, as his mother had come from their union along with an uncle whom he hadn't seen since his mother's funeral but that wasn't such a big issue within the family.

"Morning, Granda," John greeted, carefully pulling up one of the stool seats, "how are you today?"

Granda Micha turned with a great flourish at hearing the sound of his second grandsons voice and set himself off on a deep rumbling laugh, "Well well well, if it ain't my little bouncing red mongoose." Why John had been given such a nickname was beyond him but it was one of those things that you just didn't question when it came to Granda Micha. "How does the little snake eater feel today then?"

"Hungry," John said with a grin, already eyeing a large plate, full to overflowing with food. Everyone knew that Granda Micha was a great believer in using food as a remedy for everything imaginable and normally the very thought of trying to attempt one of the old man's infamous breakfasts would give the young man a stomach ache for two hours but today he felt more inclined than he had ever done to eat.

"Good, good," Granda Micha said, placing the plate in front of John, "that's a good sign indeed. Just you wait until your mama gets home, she'll be over the moon that you're eating something."

Sensibly, John began to attack the plate of bacon, sausages, pigs-in-blankets, what he could only guess to be some Jamaican style of haggis and mushrooms rather than point out once again that his mother was never returning to the caravan. It must have been some local tradition but Granda Micha always talked about his mother as if she had just popped off to the shops somewhere but it was exactly the same as with Grandma Hannah who had passed away a good ten years ago. The old man always talked about her as if she was just seeing an old friend or down at the sea front collecting shells to make necklaces to sell on market day.

That actually reminded John that he needed to go and collect some to finish off his few attempts. He wasn't going to sell them at any market; he was saving them for the Christmas tree back at his family's house in Jamaica. Finally they had been able to arrange it so that they could all go for a mad Christmas get together and John was looking forward to it.

Granda Micha grinned again at his grandson. "Enjoying it that much, are we? Always can tell with you, never shut up for a second unless you're eating something."

"That's Vincent, Granda," John said, after swallowing some of the not-quite-haggis. "You should know the difference between us now."

The old man shrugged his broad shoulders. "Heh, sometimes it gets so I can't tell the difference between all of you, curse of getting old though as Grandma Hannah will tell you there's no reason to worry about it." His deep rumbling laugh crept back in as he turned to fix up some more plates presumably for the others, "Ah, looks like they're back. Good thing too, otherwise I would have burnt all this lovely food and I can't abide such things from happening."

Shaking his head, John chuckled but kept his comments to himself and focused on munching his way through the mountain of food. Vaguely he was aware of Amberly barking loudly but he got too bemused by a lump of cheese getting caught in his teeth to really pay attention to what was going on in the rest of the kitchen. He was aware of the door opening and someone coming in but paid it no mind until a voice which he had not heard in so many years spoke directly to him.

"Oh good grief, John, you look so silly doing that," looking up, John stared at his mother in shock before sliding sideways off his chair and landing on the floor with a bump. Immediately his mother was rushing over but strangely it was not the sight of the woman he thought he would never see again which had sent the boy crashing down to the ground.

It was the fact that just for a moment; his eyes had met with an identical pair on the face of a young girl who clearly looked just as shocked as he did. Vaguely he was aware of the arms around his frame but his eyes were staring at a virtual mirror image of himself.

The girl rallied first and shook her head slightly. "Hello, John, long time no see."

Chapter 4

Twin

Staring out at the sea from the decking at the back of the caravan, Phoebe Henderson lightly clasped her pale hands together and let out a long confused but contented sigh. Today had certainly turned out to be extremely different from what she had expected and she wasn't sure how to take it. There was a boy in her life all of a sudden who had not been there before yet she knew virtually everything about him. Not just his name and the small personality details but things like the school he attended, what his teachers thought of him, days at the park and the madness of copying exactly what he wore until the age of twelve when they decided to start becoming a little more independent of one another. Yesterday none of that had existed because in her world, her twin brother had never been around. Well he had been, for about the first eighteen months of their lives but then he had been taken away to some happier place. Now he was alive and as well as could be expected and no one but her seemed aware that anything had changed.

"Oh what does this all mean?" she asked out loud, watching as a seagull startled itself with her voice and took off. "I thought wishes only came true in fairy stories, not like this."

"You made a wish?" a voice behind her said and the girl turned sharply, blue eyes glistening in fear as she regarded the boy whom looked too much like her. They still shared the same physical traits of being tall and lankly with pale skin and hair but it was a frightening thing to behold. Even dressed in a simple green summer dress and white sandals barely disguised the fact that they were identical twins of different sexes and Phoebe didn't know how to deal with the situation. Clearly John didn't either as he was shuffling about nervously as well.

Instead of covering a fact that she had already stated, the girl took a step or two closer to the boy who looked so much like her and reached out a hand attentively to touch his chest. John tensed up, taking a sharp intake of breath but allowed her to do so without much complaint. Easing her fingers forward so that the tips extended out until they became the flat of her hand, Phoebe found the heartbeat easily and felt it pounding. A smile crossed her features and a breathy laugh escaped her. Looking up at John, she nodded to him, hoping that he would get the message to do the same thing.

Gulping slowly, John mimicked the movement exactly placing the tips of his fingers on her chest and then expanding them outwards until they were flat against the chest bone. For a few seconds he wasn't sure what he felt and then suddenly there was the heartbeat, fluttering back and forth under his fingertips. It was the same heartbeat that he had heard for many years and knew it instinctively. "We really are?"

"Twins, yes," Phoebe said with a grin, feeling tears pricking at the corner of her eyes. "I never thought that I would see you ever again."

Pulling his hand back, John stepped back from the girl shaking his head. "I don't remember you… I mean, I do, but you weren't…" Stopping he took a deep breath to try and organise his thoughts. He didn't want to push the girl away but at the same time he couldn't just accept her either. Last night he had been worried about dealing with chronic sunburn and trying to keep his emotions in check over the death of his mother. Now by some astronomic chance he suddenly had his mother back and a sister, his own twin sister whom he knew nothing about.

There had never been a mention of him having a twin, though now he thought about it, his birth certificate displayed a re-issue date but he had never questioned it because his dad was so bad at filing things that they went missing all the time. It didn't make any sense in the slightest and as he stared at the girl, he just felt angry and confused. "I mean now that I'm looking at you I can think back to times in the park, the shopping sprees that used to irritate Mum no end…" he stopped and shook his head, "but even that doesn't make any sense because Mum died five years ago. I saw it happen… I was there when the car…"

"John," Phoebe said quietly, catching hold of the others hands to calm him down before shaking her head, "we need to talk about this away from the others. They don't think anything's different."

"But how can I have a twin when I've never had one?" He knew fine well that he was being horribly cruel and extremely insensitive but out of all the complicated pieces that he was trying to fit together, this was the one that made the least amount of sense. He hated not knowing or understanding things, it was one of his goals in life to never be confused or lost as far as it was humanly possible. There were some things that had no explanation but this was one that needed some form of explanation.

However the young female twin didn't appear phased by it in the slightest, instead of looking hurt or upset her blue eyes hardened into a steadfast resolve and quickly she tugged her twin down to the side of the caravan, into the shadows where no one would be looking. Thankfully there was a small awning which had been put up when they first arrived but had not as of yet been used. There was a full length mirror in it, though why was a question no one really asked and a few other odds and ends as no one had really thought of another use for the space as of yet.

"Take your shirt off," Phoebe ordered, turning away to remove the green summer dress she was wearing, though John was glad to see that she had a pair of swimming shorts and a bikini top on which reduced his nerves somewhat. He stood there for a few seconds, unsure of why he would have to remove his clothes but decided against arguing and pulled off his top. It felt strangely comfortable standing there in front of the girl who had never seen him before, which unsettled him a little but he was prepared to trust her for reasons that he did not know about yet.

"Stand in front of the mirror," Phoebe said, "and I'll show you."

Looking at his pale reflection, the blond-haired teenager didn't know quite how to react when the girl suddenly placed herself on his left hand side with the right part of her rib cage almost touching the horrible scar on his side. "Look," she said after a few moments of discomfort and slightly turned them both at an angle. Not sure what he was supposed to see, John suddenly noticed the scaring on the girl's right hand side and saw that it lined up near perfectly with his own scar.

Even though he had only read about it in books, a wave of familiarity washed over him, "We were joined?" the question sounded stupid to even his ears but he found himself automatically pulling Phoebe closer to himself as if they could be stitched back together.

"Yes, though we really baffled the doctors apparently," Phoebe said, moulding herself as best as she could against the others skin, "it's incredibly rare for conjoined twins to be different sexes."

"They separated us, didn't they?" John said, before suddenly remembering how he always cuddled up to the left hand side of his father and mother and was never happy on the right hand side, "Left hand twin, right hand twin…"

Suddenly pulling the girl into a proper hug, John held Phoebe tightly and let the sensations wash over him. Now he understood many of his little quirks and how they affected his life. He could see the little changes that made the big differences but also felt a cold stab go through his heart. "They never told me," he whispered lightly, hands gripping as gently as they could to the delicate hair. "Mum and Dad never mentioned you. That's why…"

"I guessed," Phoebe said with a smile, "they did the same with me but I went hunting for my birth certificate one day and found out the truth. They don't know about it though, I thought it best not to upset them."

John pulled back to smile at his twin before glancing towards the sound of his mother's worried voice calling for the pair of them. It was still vaguely creepy to hear. "It's strange hearing her call like that, I haven't heard her voice for over five years and yet it's still the same."

"Five years?" Phoebe asked with a frown. "There are too many similarities between our lives even though they are completely different. I think we're going to have to have a good long talk and work anything out before one of us says the wrong thing."

There was a pause in the yelling, or maybe it was just the fact that the twins were staring intently at one another. It was strange and surreal that they should be like this but suddenly a big hole in their lives had been patched up. Though the lingering thought in the back of John's mind was that this was only going to be a temporary moment in time. Though the girl with the white eyes hadn't actually spoken about how long it could be. It might only be today or it could be a week, however John found himself reasoning to himself that he wasn't in the least bit worried about such things. After all, sometimes the best moments in life were those that lasted only a short while.

"There you are," the relieved voice of their mother came filtering into the gaze and broke the spell which had fallen over the two. "I was beginning to panic! Wandering off both together with no explanation and the sun being so high, it's a wonder I didn't sprout horns and go charging off into the sunset to search high and low for the pair of you."

Neither twin spoke for a second or two before they shared an equally heartfelt grin and then launched themselves upon the unsuspecting Lucy so hard that they tumbled to the ground in a big heap of giggles. Taking in the sweet smell of fine cooked spices, baby oil and that rose scented perfume which his mother always wore; John couldn't help but cling to the woman with uttermost joy. Whereas before everything had felt unreal and doomed in some way, now this little sphere of life suddenly had a brand new meaning and he wasn't going to waste it.

"What on earth are you two little meerkats doing to your mother?" Granda Micha's voice cut into the awning as both were hugging their mother so hard the woman was brightly laughing, which had clearly disturbed the man's cooking time. "I swear the whole park can hear her laughing and we'll have the neighbours banging on our door asking us to keep quiet if we're not careful."

"Twin-thing," John and Phoebe said at the same time before looking to one another and joining in the laughter of their mother. Though only they knew the real reason behind the laughter and the impromptu hug which had come about.

Chapter 5

Mama

"Do you think I'm worrying too much, Pappas?" Lucy asked at length, leaning on the fence as she observed her children heading to the swimming pool whilst the dogs ran back and forth in their little pen, trying unsuccessfully to break out once again.

Granda Micha looked up from his current task and smiled at his only daughter. She was such the fretful thing but he could hardly blame her for being that way. Raising five children was no easy task and coupled with the events of recent years, it only made things even more difficult to bare. He stared at her posture, reading the subtle signs that showed just how tired she was but also the determination not to give in. Lucy wasn't exactly the most beautiful woman in the world, there was no way anyone could claim she would ever make it onto the cover of any famous fashion magazine but that never really troubled her.

No, his daughter was built to be practical and loving, none of this hoity toity flakiness that other woman would have adopted upon being married to a very wealthy man. There was next to no Gucci in her wardrobe just as there was no need for flashy shoes and dresses which barely appeared to fit. She did dress herself well but it was done with style and taste, the type of grown up maturity that came with maintaining one's own background and not changing her ways due to peer pressure. In fact that was what made her more beautiful than those simpering wives on the glossy magazines, because never once had Lucy Henderson denied her heritage or pretended to be anything that she wasn't.

Right now she was being what she needed to be, a worried mother who was facing yet another turning point in her life. Her father watched her appreciatively, dressed as she was in distressed jeans, a simple yellow top and her thick, wavy hair fought into a long braid which fell down the centre of her back. He couldn't see her blue eyes but knew that there was an ocean of worry in them at the moment which only brought a rolling chuckle to the old man lips, "Baby, you worry just as much as any normal mother should. Just like your Mama Hannah used to do when you were about to go off into the big wide world, it's good that you do. Shows you care."

"Papa," Lucy said with an exasperated sigh and a playful shake of her head, "you always look on the bright side of life."

Another chuckle, shorter this time responded to her statement. "Of course I do, baby, if I didn't then no one would see the light through all the darkness. Don't worry about your children, they're the right old fashioned stock and nothing and no one will harm them. You mark my words and hand me that tea towel will you?"

Passing the towel over, which was emblazed with white rabbits for some unknown reason, Lucy pondered the old man's words for a few long seconds. Her eyes lingered on his hands which were wrinkled from years upon years of washing dishes, mending fences and working long hours in the basking heat to earn a good living for his family. Even after she and Jeff had given the pair a substantial amount of money and a new house, Micha had refused to give up his job saying that he was always far happier with something to do during the day. It wasn't that he had disapproved of the money, he was overjoyed to receive it but he was a man of the earth, someone who was meant to work and not sit around on his big behind and do nothing worthwhile. His way with words always brought back a smile to Lucy's face and sometimes she wished that if even just a third of the world thought the way that her father did then it truly would be a far better place to live for everyone.

"I guess I just don't know what I'm going to do with the twins," Lucy reluctantly admitted, trying to put her thoughts into some coherent form which would at least make sense, "I mean yes they have been apart before but it could really cause problems."

Sighing, Granda Micha put the big cooking pot into the oven and closed the door before shaking his head, "Lucy, Lucy, Lucy… there you go worrying again. There's no need to worry, I can tell you that those two are going to be absolutely fine. They would have had to part ways at some point, and sure it'll be painful for them but take a look out there and see," flicking his hand back and forth towards the disappearing figures, "they are happy my little ducky, completely happy and they know that they will be apart soon. They are left twin and right twin, always have been and always will be. Look on the sunnier side of life, if they face problems they cannot grow and you can't keep them wrapped in cotton wool forever. Just relax and stop biting those nails otherwise I shall bring out Sammy the Crocodile and he will snap your fingers off and leave you in a right pickle of a situation!"

Automatically dropping her hand, Lucy stuck her tongue out at the old man before laughing, "Actually I think Diesel ate Sammy last night for supper."

"He did what?" Granda Micha started with a comical over dramatic wailing of his arms. "He cannot have eaten Sammy! That shall bring a curse down upon us all! Diesel!" The old man's voice somehow managed to raise a couple of octaves higher than it normally did as he went outside to play with the two dogs for a short time. "You had better sick up Sammy the Crocodile or he will eat his way out of your stomach and you'll end up being one dead doggy."

Laughing loudly, Lucy flopped herself down onto the sofa in the caravan and leaned on the back as she looked out to see, "Oh, Jeff, if only you were here to see all this lovely madness. Hopefully it won't be long before you awaken as well."

Chapter 6

Sammy the Crocodile

Letting the sun warm his back, Granda Micha leaned against the support beam of the decking and wiped away the sweat which had gathered on his forehead. It had certainly been an awfully long time since he had rushed around but it had transpired that Diesel and Amberly were not the typical hyperactive Springer Spaniels. In fact as far as he was concerned, they were an entire new breed of Spaniel that needed extensive monitoring else they would chew up the entire house without so much as a glance backwards. Still he couldn't help but chuckle at the pair as the tumbled back and forth in their pen, knocking about a green-coloured ball.

Micha knew fine well that the male pup hadn't eaten Sammy the Crocodile, for one thing it was far too big for the little manic creature to even begin to attempt such a thing and for another it was more than liable that the toy would have automatically snapped back. "You two are silly doggies," he smiled, his accent thick and heavy but still somehow filled with joy and mischief. "My Hannah would have adored the pair of you. She would have put you in her suitcase and taken you home if she had half the chance."

Sitting down, rather slowly, the Jamaican man looked out towards the ocean and thought lovingly of his homeland. Yes this little island was now home to him as well but even the most acclimatised person in the world can feel a little homesick at times. Amberly let out a snapping growl at her brother, deftly picked up Sammy and trotted triumphantly towards Micha before letting out a half-bark. Turning his head to the brown and white dog, who despite after having numerous baths and scrubs still looked like she was covered in mud due to her splashes of colour, the old man let out a deep rumbling laugh as he tugged the toy out of the dog's mouth, "Ah thank you, my dear, I knew you would be the one to return Sammy and save your brother from getting eaten inside out."

Picking up a ball, he threw it and watched as both dogs went chasing after it, stumbling over one another in a higgle-de-piggly motion which caused yet more laughter. "Oh, my dears, you are just the funniest things," Micha said, standing up with a grin. "I'm going to fetch your mama and she can have a good old laugh at the pair of you. She needs a good laugh these things, poor lamb, life is not being kind to her but what can one expect?"

The dogs, of course, were completely oblivious to anything that was being said and continued to wrestle for the ball back and forth whilst the old man climbed the stairs. Out of habit, his hand began tapping out a lively tune on the wooden decking and he began to sing in the most up-roaring manner but he wasn't bothered in the slightest by such things. Life and music were two essential things that had to go together. When you were happy, you were meant to sing out loud and not give two hoots about what the next door neighbours thought of you.

When times of sadness came there were songs for that too but Micha didn't sing those too often. Especially not when he was around his daughters family. Ensuring that he had the beat just right, the old man took a deep breath before bursting quite suddenly into song, singing at the top of his voice despite the fact that his daughter had fallen asleep on the couch.

"Little robin, bouncing robin, my old reggae robin. What do you do when the sun up? You dance on the branch, twang the twigs and hop hop hop it away. What do you do when the sun goes down? You dance on the ground, around and around. What do you do in the dead of night? Sleep sound sound, in your nest all right, all the way through the night. What do you do when the sun wakes up? You dance again on the old willow branch and start it all over again, little robin, little bouncing robin. The old reggae robin!" Shuffling along to the imaginary beat, Micha spotted his daughter stirring awake and carefully started brewing up some special tea. "Did my singing awaken the pretty little robin?"

"Just about," Lucy groaned, rubbing her eyes to get rid of the sleep in them, "when did I fall asleep?"

Micha didn't reply for a few seconds, as he was in the process of bouncing around the tiny kitchen flipping the ingredients around to make the tea. "Around an hour or two ago, I've been keeping your doggies amused and thought you should see their antics. It'll have you laughing in no time," her father said, pouring some hot water over the carefully selected leaves, "but I thinks that this will help to wake up the slumbering mind."

Taking the tea from the old man, Lucy sniffed it appreciatory and sighed, "What would I ever do without you around, Papa?"

"Probably get yourself into a big tangle with the nearest monkey tree like you used to do all the time when you were a kiddie," replied her father with an all knowing grin, "the amount of times I told you to stay out of that blooming thing and yet you still insisted in climbing up it every other day."

Letting out a smile, Lucy shook her head and stared in no particular direction for a short while. She remembered her childhood, how she had once been a raving tomboy who would think of nothing more than running into a muddy puddle, clambering up trees, making dens out of cardboard and a thousand and one other insane things that she used to do. Even when she went off to university to study and fell in love with her one and only beloved man in the entire world, she still held that firm independence which marked her out. Despite the fact that she had given birth to five children, she was still very much a tomcat though even she was aware of the fact that over the last couple of years that side of her had faded.

"Paps," she asked at length, "am I making a mistake?"

Raising an eyebrow at his daughter, Micha shook his head. "No, babe, you're not making no mistakes. You're just worried is all… a lot has happened to you all over the last few years and it's taking its toll. It's perfectly natural for a mother to fret like this; you'll get over it all someday I promise you that." Sitting down next to his girl, he pulled her into a one armed hug whilst carefully dropping some rum into the tea. "That ought to be enough to pick you up and make you feel better, my dear."

"Papa!" Lucy said whilst playfully digging her father in the ribs. "I can't drink this and then go driving."

Micha gave his daughter a look which clearly said what he thought of that sentence, "Order a taxi and have a good time. You can't be Little Miss Responsible all the time, you know. Have a drink or two, or three or four," his dark eyes glimmered with that prospect, "and come back here raving drunk. I'll tip you into the bath, soak you through and then shove you to bed. Just like I always used to do with your mama. Trust me, it'll do you a world of good."

"And give me the worlds worse hangover," Lucy said with a smile before shaking her head. "I suppose I could give it a go. I'm sure there'll be at least someone there who will help me down a few bottles."

Micha just chuckled. "Too true, my girl, too true. Oh I got Sammy back!"

Lucy recoiled in disgust. "Ah! Papa, he's covered in dog drool! That's horrible!" However she couldn't help but bring forth a chuckle of her own. "I swear you're the strangest father in the entire world!"

"Ah but they'll never be another one like me," Micha said with a grin, preparing to dodge out of the way of the approaching dogs, "never in a million years. Lucy, duck!"

At that precise moment, Amberly and Diesel leapt forward and tackled Lucy with slobbering wet licks. Micha just quietly moved out of the way and went to check that the children's clothes were ready for tonight. He was sure they would try to find some way to not wear them but that wasn't going to happen on his watch, without a doubt it wouldn't.

Chapter 7

Swimming Pool

"I swear to—" Scott managed to successfully stop himself from swearing aloud in this very public place. "Alan, if you don't get down from there this instant I swear I will come and rip you to pieces."

The youngest Henderson had managed to somehow climb all the way to the top of an artificial palm tree and was gleefully hanging upside down from it. His tongue was pointed directly at Scott and his little hands were waving back and forth madly, "Nehy! Scotty, can't get me!" he chanted back and forth like all children of a certain age do when they believe that they have the upper hand. Just rather unfortunately in this situation, Alan did because there was no way the lifeguards were going to allow someone like Scott to clamber up the tree in order to get his wayward brother down.

How else they expected the elder to do so was a complete mystery but thankfully the lifeguards were distracted by a bunch of school children who had decided to invade the deep end of the pool. "Scotty will get very mad at you if you don't come down," Scott shouted back up to the figure, growling a little as his attempts to catch the boy failed when the spirited little devil nimbly avoided his fingers, "you could hurt yourself!"

"Alan won't hurt himself," the boy replied, reasoning in his six-year-old logic which was usually about as much help as reading a book back to front and upside down. "Alan never hurts himself when climbing trees."

Scott growled and went to pounce once again on the scrambling boy but found himself flanked by the twins who had identical grins on their faces. For a second he thought of shouting at them too but found Phoebe tugging him lightly away from the scene whilst John looked up completely innocently at his brother, "Are you not going to come down at all?"

"Nope!" came the reply from the thick blob of golden hair he could just see in amongst the leaves. "I'm going to stay here and never come down."

"Really?" John knew this old game so well he could have recited it in his sleep but it was one of those things that had to be done in order to maintain some form of resemblance to normal life. Of course with the Henderson's, normality conceited of constant mayhem but it was their lot in life and that was all that they needed. "Not even for a double chocolate milkshake and kids box from the canteen?"

There was a pause for a fraction of a second; clearly the younger was thinking this over, "Can I have cake?"

"If there is some then, yes, you can," John said but seeing the mad look upon his brother's face, tactfully remembered to add on the punishment. "Though you will have to apologise to Scott for being such a naughty boy and then tell Mum and Granda what you did when we got home."

"And not eat any pudding right?" Alan answered half-way down the trunk of the tree with amazing grip and balance for someone his age.

John nodded but left Scott to chase the young scallywag to the canteen because he had done way too much running already today. Keeping an eye on Alan was like trying to herd a particularly dim flock of sheep through a tight ravine. The youngster had the attention span of a gnat at the best of times and could be relied upon to go chasing after some bright thing or other like a magpie. If he wasn't running then he was playing and if he wasn't playing he was making a den or more correctly a mess.

Phoebe just chuckled as she fell into step with her twin, watching as the eldest and the youngest managed to somehow make complete fools of themselves with absolutely no one complaining. It was a strange thing indeed that such an age range could be built upon with next to no hassle but that was just the way that things went in this family. Linking fingers with her twin, she smiled happily, "Do you think those two could make a pretty good comedy duo or am I just reading too much into this whole situation?"

"Ha, those two have nothing on Vincent when he gets going," John said, referring to the missing brother in the family whom presumably was still off in the wide world performing in some concert, "all the press says that he's a well-mannered boy whose always polite and well refined. I swear that he just does it in order to annoy us all the more when he comes home." Though his words were spoken lightly and with a slight laughter tinged edge, there was still a stabbing sensation which went through his heart as he thought of the middle brother. There was no way that anyone would ever dream of denying that the other wasn't anything but an extraordinary singer and performer, it was just the fact that sometimes his absence was felt in the house.

Well, when they were actually at home for any length of time these days. What with Jeff's recent job promotion and access to a whole lot more funds, the man had hit upon the idea of buying a new home for his ever growing family. However instead of thinking slightly sensibly like a normal father would do, their father had big ideas and wanted to explore the world first to find just where fitted right for everyone. He seemed rather oblivious to the fact that Scott was due to head off to university within the next couple of weeks. Vincent was touring the world as he became a much more recognised household name after winning a very public talent competition and John himself was due to go off to America in order to study at a school which would mean that he wouldn't be around. Pretty soon there would only be Alan and Jeff, plus the two hyperactive dogs, to worry about, but it was more than likely just the way that the other was dealing with things.

Blinking at just how extraordinarily stupid he had just been, John glanced at Phoebe and wondered just what this reality held for them all. Yes his mother was around, that much was plain to see and it seemed that no matter which realm of reality he was in Granda Micha was still the maddest and coolest Grandfather on the block but it had taken him a moment or two to realise that Jeff had not appeared insofar. Maybe he was just out and about, he remembered that from his younger years but just somehow it didn't feel quite right. Plus it more than likely wasn't a good time to be trying to piece together the pieces of a very complicated puzzle which still was only just beginning to take shape. Instead he decided to ask something that would at least make sense to the girl but wouldn't appear out of context to the others if they should overhear.

"Phoebe?" he asked, dodging nimbly a group of kids who were squealing their way down towards the pool much to their mother's dismay. "Are we going to the garden party that Miss Penny is holding today?"

Looking across at her brother, the blonde-haired girl looked confused for a few seconds but then grinned. "Yeah, we're going. I'm pretty sure that Scott's going to finally ask her out after all these years but it might just take a good old fashioned shove to get him to do so despite the fact that it's painfully obvious to everyone." Just to prove that sometimes even the gods of fate like to have a bit of a laugh and a joke on, Scott happened to trip at that precise moment and almost tumbled down a flight of stairs.

He turned to glare at his twin siblings but said nothing, just pointing to a table because he knew instinctively what they would want to eat. John had to bite his tongue until the other was safely out of earshot before bursting into laughter. "That was good," he commented happily.

"I know, wasn't it just?" Phoebe grinned back, stretching her pale arms upwards to get a little bit of movement in them as she hadn't done so in a while. "There is one thing I'm not looking forward to about the party though."

Tilting his head to the side in question, the male twin caught a glimmer of joy in the blue orbs which were his sister's eyes.

"Mum's insisting that I wear a proper dress and I don't want to do so in the slightest."

Frowning, John couldn't comprehend why this was a bad thing but opted for a different tactful approach to answering. "You were wearing one earlier, what's the difference?"

For a moment Phoebe wondered what had gotten into John but then remembered that strictly speaking in her world he had been dead until this morning. She had better get used to this sort of odd occurrence which might overstep the boundaries of normal conversation but there were things that needed to be done and sorted out. Blowing breath out from beneath her teeth, the girl shook her head. "That dress is different. Grandma made it for me when I was young. But the dress that Mum wants me to wear is all... well..."

"Absolutely stunning and gorgeous," cut in Scott, returning with a plastic tray filled with food and drink. "You'll be the prettiest girl at the ball and you're not getting out of wearing it either."

"Scott!" Phoebe whined. "I look like some decoration that belongs on the top of a cake in that dress. Mum's just making me wear it to show off."

Scott glared dangerously at his sister. "If you think Mum's dolling you up for that reason alone you've got to realign your thinking, sis." Sighing, he waved a cheeseburger in her general direction but hardly paused for finding the correct explanation for everything, "Look I know you're worried about that prat of an ex of yours being around but I can assure you that if he is, he's going to have me, John, Alan and possibly Diesel to deal with. Don't let that bugger bother you anymore my girl, he had no right to say what he did to you and no way in any version of hell is he ever going to get the one up on you ever again."

Watching Phoebe carefully picking at her salad, John got the impression that someone had deliberately hurt the girl a while ago and felt anger boiling through his system. No one had the right to do anything like that to any girl and especially not his twin sister. Catching hold of the girl's hand, he locked eyes with her, fierce and deadly, "If he turns up tonight, you just point him out to me Phoebe and I'll knock him into the middle of next week."

Chapter 8

Getting Ready

"Phoebe Henderson!" Lucy's sharp voice cut across the general quiet of the caravan as the children were getting ready. "You are not going to the party in that! We've already had this discussion young lady and I'm not going through it again."

"But, Mum!" the young girl protested through the closed door. "I can't wear something like that! I'll become the laughing stock of the entire party."

There was an audible sigh from their mother as John helped Alan with the complicated button array on his shirt. He understood well enough that they were going to a very posh party but why there was the need for the full button-down suits was a bit of a worrying question. Scott wasn't helping in the slightest by keeping himself very much out of the way, having claimed the bathroom a good twenty minutes ago, and had as of yet to remove himself. "There we go," he said to his youngest brother, "now go and see Granda and he'll do something with that mop of yours."

"It's not a mop!" Alan tried to contest, deliberately running his little fingers through his hair in order to mess it up even more. Rolling his eyes, John just lightly pushed the boy forward knowing fine well that the youngster didn't mind his Granda doing his hair and glanced towards the opposite door. Granted, he was nowhere near ready yet, having only a pair of trousers on and his shirt only half buttoned but he wanted to find out what all the fuss was about. By the way that Phoebe was going on, it almost sounded as if she were being forced to some form of debutante ball dress but there had to be more of a reason to it than that.

Vaguely, he tried to recall some of the events of a non-existent childhood to his mind but found that he could only really recall until around the age of nine years old. The teenage years were missing which was probably just a side effect of the whole two realities thing but it didn't appear to affect anyone but him which was more than slightly worrying. Shaking his head, the blond decided to stop thinking about it and instead focus on helping his twin out of a predicament which clearly she did not like to be in.

Without even pausing to knock on the door, he opened it and went into the room. Unlike most normal situations like this where there would be a great deal of shouting and him being shoved out of the room, Phoebe just looked up at him with a slightly questioning expression not caring apparently that she was sitting in front of her twin in nothing but her underwear. Strangely John found that he wasn't bothered by her appearance either, normally even the very mention of a pair of knickers had the young boy in bright red blushes that were worse than any sunburn for hours. Maybe it was because the girl was his twin and they had shared so much that it wasn't that embarrassing. Plus, the reminder of the scar on her right hand side gave him a fair guess as to why he wasn't that fussed. They had been born joined together, so instinctively they knew one another's bodies intimately. Granted they had both grown recently and there was nothing that could deny that small factor but it still felt perfectly normal to him. "What's all the yelling about? You can't be that averse to wearing a dress, twin." A shudder of joy went through his system at being able to say that word though he didn't quite understand as to why.

Phoebe scowled at her brother, her eyes looking slightly livid as she huffed, "I'm not that adverse! I just don't want to wear that thing."

John turned to look at the dress which clearly his mother had picked out in earnest for the girl and immediately knew what was wrong with it. It wasn't that it wasn't absolutely stunning, with its fine lines and satin light colour, nor was it anything to do with the trimming and the embroidery. Most girls would have gladly thrown themselves upon this dress because it was utterly stunning and completely beautiful. Almost the perfect princess dress of any fantasy that any girl could have ever wanted. However for Phoebe it was the wrong dress for the simple fact that the girl had never wanted to be a princess in her entire life and the one and only time she had been, it had ended in near disaster.

A memory stirred in his head, old and faded like he was watching it on some black and white television set that was on the point of breaking. They were at a school fate with all the trimmings and a whole host of different competitions. He remembered it well from his own perspective because it had been the first time that he had won the science award for his own international space station with working rocket that flew into the sky and then could be radio controlled to do all sorts of moves. Now he looked back upon that day, he remembered that Phoebe had entered the 'Princess' fancy dress costume and had gone in a lovely deep pink dress with gold and silver effect embroidery, her hair tied up in a sweeping pony-tail and fake silver tiara. She had looked absolutely lovely and was clearly one of the winners from the outset.

But then when the actual parade came about, Phoebe was nowhere to be found and John had immediately panicked. They searched for the girl in the hopes that she had just got lost and it was only just after all the awards had been given out that one of the teachers hurried up to Lucy to advise that she had been found. Racing to the hall, they had discovered the little girl in tears, dress ruined beyond comprehension, covered in mud and some wicked child had viciously cut her hair off with a rough pair of scissors. John knew who it was and got into trouble the next day for roughing the girl up but he hadn't cared. He had been grounded of course for such a thing but secretly his parents had been proud of him and were even happier when the parents of the girl's responsible had agreed to pay for the wrecked dress and also the medical bill as Phoebe had been pushed down a set of stairs and broken a rib.

Kneeling in front of the much now older girl, John took her hands and rubbed his thumbs across the back of them. "It's okay. Those girls aren't going to be there tonight, there's no way that they would get in with Penny's lot."

Staring at her twins, Lucy let out a sigh of disbelief, "Oh my... babes, you should have said and I wouldn't have bought you it. God, I'm such a fool." Wrapping herself around her daughter, the mother wondered what to do now considering the fact that they really didn't have the time to go and get another dress. Maybe they could do some quick alterations but even that was a risky business. Worriedly she bit her lip, looking to John for advice and guidance, surprised to see the boy thinking things through.

Suddenly John got up and winked. "I'm just going to check on something, be right back." The pair watched the left twin leave before looking at each other and Lucy ran her hands through Phoebe's long hair.

"We really are a right pair aren't we, sweetheart?"

"Yeah," Phoebe nodded, looking down at the ground. "I'm sorry I didn't say something sooner… I just don't like going back through that memory."

Kissing the top of her daughter's head, the light haired woman nodded. "I understand, my dear, just what we're going to do now though is beyond me."

Thankfully there was someone who knew exactly what had to be done and John knew that there was a very high chance that he could save the day. Turning onto the decking, he grinned upon seeing Granda Micha sitting on a chair with a cup of tea holding down the newspaper and a pen in his hand. "Hey, Granda," John opened, knowing that it would get the old man's attention, "can I ask you something?"

"As long as you can help me with this blasted puzzle, it's driving me up the wall." Clearly, the elder was too absorbed in his current brain activity for the day and wouldn't be budging from the spot until it was complete or he got too tired of it. "What's 'a cure'? Six letters."

"Remedy," John said quickly, used to helping out with crosswords and other such puzzles on a daily basis. "Do you still keep some of Grandma Hannah's dresses here?"

Raising his head after he finished writing, Granda Micha looked at his second grandson with interest. Slowly an eyebrow rose as he tried to work out the need before a typical deep rumble began, "Why yes I do. I take it your mama's remembered about that whole princess thing with Phoebe's then?"

Nodding in response, John helped his grandfather up out of the seat and followed the man down to the next caravan. Why Granda Micha still kept his caravan here was something of a mystery but it was always a handy place to catch the aged figure if he wasn't at home. He said he liked it here and it gave him great courage to go on and keep up with the world. Vincent was convinced it was because he was having a fling with the widow down at caravan number nine but there was no proof of that in the slightest and it was probably a good thing to.

Going inside, the warm smells of incense, spices and home cooking nearly knocked the poor boy out but Granda Micha just kept on going until he reached the bedroom and delicately ran his hand across the dark wood of the wardrobe, "Don't mind us, Hannah, my dear, we're just getting your granddaughter out of a fix… as well as your bonny bell."

Opening the door revealed a selection of dresses that ranged from the most elegant ball gowns to proper rockers outfits to the most whacked out and craziest dresses that had ever been seen. Grandma Hannah wasn't known for being subtle in the slightest and had all sorts of really mad ideas when it came to looking good but always managed to somehow pull it off perfectly. However there was only one dress that John wanted and he smiled upon spotting it in-between a bright pink Flapper Dress and something that rightly belonged in *The Rocky Horror Picture Show*.

Carefully picking it out, he removed the protective dry clean plastic and smiled joyfully at it. It was a just off pastel green sleeveless knee length dress with a darker green nature print over the top though it was spaced out evenly and didn't dominate everything. It was made of a fine satin and was ridged around the end to give it a bit more shape. There was a green petticoat, lacy and fully covering with a white sleeved overcoat that was just trimmed to fit around the wearer's waist. He was pretty sure that Phoebe had some shoes that would go with it as well as tights and accessories and it was just the type of thing to suit the young girl. He smiled at Granda Micha, "This looks like it was made for Phoebe, when did Grandma wear this?"

"On our first date," the old man smiled fondly at the memory, "and on the day that you two were christened in the Jamaican church. She said that one day Phoebe would wear it and I think you've definitely made the best choice. Though I'm surprised that you didn't go for the red dress, your Granny used to look a million dollars in it."

John smiled at the old man. "Unfortunately with our complexion, Granda, red makes us look like a clown gone very wrong."

Chapter 9

The Party

Penelope Christina Elkins' house was roughly the size of a fairly roomy estate in any town. It housed the main house which upon itself was actually very modest for being owned by one of the world's most exclusive children, being only three storeys with about five rooms maximum. Of course there were some luxuries, along the lines of a personal swimming pool with Jacuzzi attached and a tennis ground nearby but it was done to match the theme of the house. It was all tasteful and refined, elegant and beautiful yes but with a practical purpose which made it work on many different levels. It was the sort of thing you would expect to find in an old money family, an heirloom passed down through the generations, but Penelope, or Penny as everyone who got to know her called her, did not come from such a background.

She was one of those people who appeared oddly blessed with the greatest amount of luck ever. Starting life as a girl living in a rough council estate, she had clearly always been ahead in the world of the others and instead of getting fascinated in the world of gossip, looking older than what you legally should do and the most forbidden substance of all – boys – Penny had decided that she was going to be an actress. Never the one to set her sights low, she made a pledge that she would star in a world class movie and become a shimmering screen siren. So far her resume consisted of three international films which had skyrocketed out of all proportions, two years touring with The Royal Shakespeare Company and her latest project was for a dazzling stage production of some book which evaded John's memory right now.

Despite her ever growing personal profile, Penny had always remained firmly loyal to her roots, and whilst she most certainly had spent a lot of money on her own house she had given a majority of it back to her parents and local community. She really was a darling to behold and never once believed that it would last forever, she was just enjoying the life that she had been blessed with. Plus trying desperately to get a certain Scott Henderson to finally actually go out with her with the long term aim of being able to marry him. She had declared her love for him when they were thirteen years old and now that both were nineteen it was starting to get to the point where realistically they needed to work it all out.

Sitting in a white wooden chair, John watched as his brother and presumable sister-in-law of the future flirted unashamedly by the water fountain. Absolutely no press were around and any sneaking paparazzi were being manhandled out of the way by an ever present personal force who quietly reminded them of their place in Penny's world. As he watched, John smiled, understanding fully why Scott was attracted to the starlet. She was smaller than he was and built with a pleasing figure that lent itself to grace and poise rather than beauty but her dazzling smile, thick strawberry-blonde hair which was worn up in a high pony-tail tonight and amazing chocolate brown eyes that made anyone who beheld them want to melt into a very happy gooey mess, all added to the picture as a whole. Penny was a classic beauty, one that could age gracefully and naturally and not be afflicted with the need to constantly use chemicals on herself to stop aging.

However, she wasn't the type to get by on just her looks; she was a genuine fine actress who could out-do virtually any of the Hollywood bimbos that they kept on trying to push on the screen. John's smile deepened as he saw Scott place a hand tenderly on her cheek and moved just a little closer but politely turned away. He knew that the humiliation of being observed by a relative and wasn't about to bestow it upon his elder brother.

"You haven't happened to see Alan around have you?" His mother's voice cut into his thoughts and John looked up in slight surprise. It was still extremely strange to hear her voice, sometimes he thought that he was just imaging all of this and nothing was really happening but it was far too real for it to be something like that.

Lightly, he shook his head in response to her question. "I'm afraid not, I thought he had run off to play with some friends from school."

"Friends from?" Lucy started, tilting her head up to the sky so that her hair glimmered in the fading light. "Ah, I know where he's gone. The little rascal. Thank you, John."

Watching as she left, the swirls of her dark grey skirt catching the tips of the grass the boy just shook his head and chuckled. "Never could keep an eye on us all could you?" he murmured lightly to himself before nearly jumping out of his skin as he found Paul, Penny's personal chauffeur and possibly elder brother but no one had ever been able to confirm or deny such things, standing right next to him. "Geez, will you not do that. You're like some ninja with the way you can sneak up on people so quietly."

Paul raised a finely sculpted eyebrow at the young man before smiling faintly. "I did not sneak up on you sir, I merely arrived by your side and you did not notice the fact."

Glaring only slightly at the other for pointing out the obvious truth of the situation, John rolled his eyes. "I still say that you're a sneaky ninja."

"Miss Phoebe requests your company, sir." Paul didn't even pause to comment upon begin called a ninja once again, he always got it from various younger members of the Henderson family. "It appears that she is getting some unwanted attention and since Scott is currently busy with Miss Penny."

"I get the picture," John said, standing up and stretching only slightly as he had been sitting down for far too long. "Where is she?"

Bowing his head low, Paul pointed in the girl's general direction with his palm up and facing outwards. "She is in the rose garden, sir. Do you wish me to accompany you?"

Shaking his head, the young albino boy took a quick look around the garden before spotting an all too familiar scene about to take place. "No I will be all right, but you may want to catch the young fellow who's attempting to climb the statue over there."

Looking up sharply, Paul turned his attention to the aforementioned child, who for once thankfully wasn't Alan, and was quickly marching off towards the boy with all the intention of a speeding train. Taking a deep breath, John quickly set along the path to the rose garden and wondered who on earth would be giving Phoebe unwanted attention. Yes he had to admit that she was one extremely pretty young lady but normally she could tell a boy off without even upsetting him in the slightest.

Instead of worrying about it, he followed the path and was only vaguely aware of a black car sitting in the drive way. There were plenty of people around these days who drove in cars with blacked out windows and there were a few people at the party who clearly believed that this was a necessity for themselves so he didn't think anything odd about it in the slightest.

Turning around a corner, John spotted a lean figure with a mop of very stylish black hair, white shirt and black trousers leaning exceptionally close to Phoebe. Actually if truth be told he was actually resting his head upon her lap and the girl hardly appeared bothered by him at all. They were sitting on a garden swing which lightly moved back and forth in a gentle swaying motion and everything seemed at peace. "Sis?" John asked at length, approaching the pair with a confused expression.

Twisting her head around to John, Phoebe just smiled and held out her hand. "Come and see who I've got here."

Taking the offered hand with an even more confused stare, John carefully stepped around to the front of the swing and took a long hard look at the sleepers face. It was well defined with strong cheek bones and a slightly darker tone than he normally displayed. An ear-ring glimmered on the sleeping boy's left ear as the sun faded for the day, and just visible was a small white scar underneath his right eye. It had been from a boating accident when they were young and it was nothing short of a miracle that the boy hadn't lost the whole eye with how close the blade came to slicing it open.

Suddenly leaping forward, John tickle-attacked the boy on his stomach, knowing that he was extra sensitive around that area and was immediately rewarded with a long peal of laughter from the other. "If you think I'm going to fall for that trick twice, Vincent, you've got another thing coming, you little sod!" he said, keeping up the tickling for a few seconds before suddenly finding himself enveloped in a big bear hug from his younger brother which had them both toppling backwards onto the ground with a comical sounding thump.

"Ha!" Vincent said, grinning cheekily. "But you're still not old enough to not fall for that one! Just you wait till I tell Mum that I got you, she'll laugh herself silly. Plus it's Vince thank you very much."

John felt like making a comment about that name sounding like a meat product but opted against it. Instead he pushed the other off him before standing up and hauling the just turned fourteen-year-old into a firm brotherly hug. "I think you'll find that she smothers you in more kisses than she's ever done before. So would Dad if he were here." That was still a point of contention that the older boy had to work out because he just presumed that his father was away on a business trip.

Vincent gave an awkward little laugh and hung his head a little but somehow managed to smile. "Yeah, I'm sure he would. Now let's go find the rest of them, I can't wait to tell you about everything I've been doing."

Rushing off, Vincent bit back his negative emotions about being reminded about their father. He knew that it was just John's way of dealing with things, as he tended to copy Granda Micha's way of thinking but it was still a very raw subject with the younger teenager.

Turning to look at his twin, who also looked a little uncomfortable, John suddenly felt a bit on the sorry side for speaking like he had done. "Where is Dad?"

Phoebe looked up at him with sad eyes before shaking her head. "It's better that you don't know, John. Much better that you don't." Taking his hand, the pair walked towards the figure of Vincent who had stopped to wait for them with that bright smile of his plastered on his face. Realising that maybe he had struck the wrong nerve, John ruffled the others hair as his way of apologising and received a series of complaints from the younger but taller boy. Not that he was going to complain of course, anything was better than an upset Vincent.

Though he did have to wonder about what had happened, maybe his father was dead in this world which would make some form of sense but then John felt guilty about being able to detach himself from it that much. Plus there were other questions that were running through his mind as well, as the more he thought about it the more he realised that something was very off about this situation. If him and Phoebe had really been conjoined twins when they were born, surely they should have been the same. Yes they shared the same condition, physical appearance and other such things but there was no way that they could be brother and sister. Twin brothers or twin sisters were possible but to be conjoined could not create two separate sexes.

His mind filtered back to the re-issued birth certificate he had found, maybe that had some of the answers that he was looking for. Mentally he placed that thought in the back of his mind and decided to enjoy the fact that Vincent was back with them for now. He could always talk to Phoebe about it later on.

Chapter 10

Presents

"And I swear there were all these girls and they were just throwing themselves at the stage in a frantic panic." Vincent was gaily swinging his arms around like a mad thing, expressing the situation with rather dynamic movements as well as vocally, "I really thought that someone was going to get hurt and all I had done was step onto the stage and smile."

Scott grinned, having joined up with the group with Penny on his arm. "I never thought the day would come when my younger twerp of a brother would beat me in the good looks department."

"As far as I'm concerned," Penny cut in with her very smooth British accent that was only just lined with a bit of a Cornish twang, "he hasn't surpassed you in the slightest."

Vincent frowned and glanced to John for an explanation who simply shook his head, thankfully Penny realised what she had said and quickly corrected herself. "Oh but, Vince, you're still going to be my cute little bunny boy no matter what happens."

"Are you two going out now or what?" Ever the one to be straight to the point, Vincent had pretty much just hit the nail on the head in regards to the whole situation but most of the assembled group just let it slide. A blind man on a horse travelling backwards could quite clearly see that Scott had finally gotten around to the whole 'let's make this official' situation and was virtually glowing with pride. Looking around the rest of the faces of the group, Vincent guessed that he had got it in one but nobody else was going to comment on it, so he swapped to a much safer topic of conversation. "Where's Mum anyway? Normally she's..."

Before the boy could finish his sentence he was suddenly bundled up into a great big loving hug that hoisted him off the floor. Despite being just an inch or two taller than his mother, she was still perfectly able to lift him clean off the floor and spin him around like he was a two-year-old all over again. "Oh my! Vinny, I've missed you so much! Why don't you ever return the letters I send you," as per usual, Lucy's self-control and restraint went completely out of the window as she started smothering the boy in kisses whilst still hugging him.

"Mam! Get off me!" Vincent playfully growled at his over-affectionate mother. "Look it's only been two months since you last saw me! You're ruining my image."

"And since when has it been inappropriate for a mother to not fuss over her son?" Lucy countered immediately, still holding him tight. "You could have at least called us to let us all know you were coming."

Whilst the pair continued to fuss over one another, Vincent was definitely the mummy's boy of the family. John looked across at Phoebe whom he was sitting next to. "Two months ago? He wasn't back then, was he?"

"No, she went out to see one of his shows. Unfortunately it was right in the middle of school term and you know what she's like for ensuring that we stay and do the time." Whispering lightly the girl smiled at her twin before glancing back at the happy pair. For a few seconds John was quiet, thinking about the difference from the world that he knew. The last time he had attended one of Vincent's concerts was last year when the whole family had gone across to Japan because the musical one of the family was taking part in a pretty big show at the time. Vaguely he wondered why his mother had been the only one to go to this other show but pushed the thought to the side of his mind.

It had become apparent that whilst the Henderson family were still fairly well off in this reality, it was not quite to the same level as it was back with his own. Maybe the mysterious absence of his father could explain that one but really there was nothing else to try and make things add up. Still lightly the boy shook his head and chuckled. "She's not going to let go of you now you realise, Vince?" The blond smiled. "You'll be lucky if you make it back to your beloved fan girls."

Rolling his dark green eyes the younger brother scowled at the thought before kneeling to catch the charging Alan and hoist him up. "I still wish it were more fan boys to be truthful."

Phoebe chuckled at the comment. "Yeah, has Kimura forgiven you for that kiss yet?"

It had been well known within the family that Vincent was gay, for a number of years. It had started when for Christmas when he was age five he had asked for a Ken and Barbie Dream house with a couple of dolls to play with. It had come as a bit of a shock but eventually they had accepted it for what it was and

74

things ran much smoother. As soon as the young man had gone off to Japan to stay with a distant relative and auditioned for one of the agencies out there, he had been snapped up almost instantly. Being tall, with a richly dark skin, dark green eyes and slick black hair he had pretty quickly become one of the most desired male junior artists but had always kept his sexuality hidden. Kimura was one of the boys that he frequently appeared with and during one song, Vincent had accidentally-on-purpose kissed the other, mainly for a bit of fan service but also to satisfy one of his many crushes.

Insofar as anyone knew, Kimura was still not talking to the other and the magazines were rife with stories about fights and all sorts. Vincent had apologised openly of course and was still in the process of trying to convince the other that he hadn't meant it but that was as far as anyone really knew what was going on. Vincent for his part, when the question was raised, managed to blush profoundly and half-hid his face in the crook of Alan's neck, unaware that this gave the six-year-old the perfect opportunity to start smearing his caramel covered hands all through the other's hair.

"I take that as a no?" Phoebe probed with a grin and an evil little chuckle which was shared by her twin.

For a few seconds, Vincent looked a little awkward. "Well... kind of but not... it's still a bit on the... I don't really know... Alan, will you stop wrecking my hair!" Holding the young boy out at arm's length he glared at the youngster, who just stuck his tongue out at him in return before trying to wriggle free.

"But hair is supposed to be messy!" the youngest blond replied. "It is in all the videos!"

Lucy plucked Alan away from his slightly annoyed brother's arms and chuckled. "Alan, you've got a lot to learn dear."

Penny chuckled. "Oh just you wait, in a couple of years he'll be chasing after the girls and then there will be absolute hell going on."

"Did you have to remind me of that?" Lucy groaned before chuckling lightly and plopping herself down onto a nearby seat with a sigh. "Honestly, you lot are going to drive me so far up the wall one day."

"Good thing I've got just the thing to cheer you up then!" Already back in his happy-go-lucky self-esteem mode, Vincent waved over one of his PAs – there was something slightly strange about a fourteen-year-old having a PA but there was next to no point in arguing over such things – who was carrying a selection of boxes. "Since I'm pretty sure that I've missed everyone's birthday, Easter and last Christmas I thought it was high time that I bring back presents for everyone."

There was a chorus of ohhs and awws from the entire group and soon there were a lot of straggles of wrapping paper, bubble wrap and sticky tape all over the small section of garden that the family had commandeered for themselves. Clearly the boy had put a lot of thought into each present, choosing different elements of the receiver's personality in order to match the present up with the correct event but with his own unique twist on things.

For his mother, Vincent bought a fine white gold necklace trimmed and layered in thick binding loops for her birthday, the Christmas gift of a beautifully crafted Bonsai Tree which had been preserved in crystal for all eternity and for Easter, as it was the traditional routine of buying a joke present he had gotten her a book entitled 'Fifty-One Ways to Burn Dinner and Get Away with It'.

Scott much to his delight and dismay received a brand new digital watch which spoke aloud the time in a very irritating voice which was fluent in Japanese only and was conveniently without the manual so switching the mode off was going to be a tricky thing to do, but it was an interesting birthday present no one could deny that. For Christmas he had a much better received gift of an iPad that had plenty of applications to download as well as a Skype phone for when he was going to be away. His Easter present was unfortunately rather predictable as it was in the form of a combat Action Man doll with a selection of army-themed accessories.

Possibly the easiest member of the family to buy for was Alan as his current favourite television shows consisted of giant robots fighting one another and a boy who could turn into several different types of aliens through the power of a watch. So for his birthday he had received a copy of the watch which emitted the sounds of the aliens as well as the masks to go with them so that he could charge merrily about making the correct noise for the correct monster. The Christmas box was nearly as big as the six-year-old and contained a huge stuffed dinosaur robot plushi which roared loudly whenever it's stomach was pressed, or yelled 'I am King' alternatively. The Easter Joke for Alan was a book entitled 'The young man's compendium of life' which had lots of ways for a young gentleman to behave himself. Being too young to really understand, Alan had amused himself by playing with the squishy dinosaurs which came with the present.

The twins received presents that, as per usual, were joint in some form or other. John didn't quite understand the logic at first, until he remembered that when they had been little they had always received gifts which either matched or could be linked. Therefore the Christmas present for the pair of them was a very long and glorious knitted scarf, with one half being blue and green for John and the other being pink and purple for Phoebe which joined together by Velcro straps. It could be separated which was a good thing but it still did look a little on the odd side. The joke Easter present was probably the best one that they had received in a long time. It was a single candle light which had a series of interchangeable shades to go on top of it that spun around to create different sources of light or shapes on the walls or other silly things along those lines. When asked why they had received such an odd thing, Vincent had sheepishly said, "Well last time I talked to Mum, she said you two still had trouble sleeping and that the last night light you had got busted accidentally so I thought it would be a good replacement."

It wasn't that the twins were afraid of the dark, par say; it was just that they didn't like it very much. For some reason the absence of light of any form would cause them to feel uneasy and make them prone to nightmares that sent shudders down their spines. If they did try to sleep when it was pitch dark then they would suffer from horrible nightmares about burning in the sunlight into clouds of dust so the night light was always there to keep things even. The last one that they had was a very old thing when it was bought and was in the shape of a mushroom house with a chimney, windows and rabbits tending to the garden. It was supposedly based off the old Braer Rabbit stories or something along those lines and had unfortunately been knocked off its table one day when the hoovering was being done.

Thankfully their birthday presents were completely separate which was a good thing and once again Vincent proved that despite the fact he spent a majority of the year away from his family, he still knew them far better than anyone would really have guessed. Since he had actually missed two of the twins birthdays, due to a sudden concert announced in the December about a week before hand, they had two presents apiece and both were themed around them explicable. John received a very fine and powerful telescope which had several interchangeable lenses on it for seeing far greater distances, and an astronavigation book which included extremely detailed star charts and was signed by Patrick Moore, the man responsible for getting John interested in space all those years ago. Granted he had first seen the man as the infamous Gamesmaster on the television show of the very same name but he had expanded his knowledge since then and dutifully recorded every show and watched them back time and time again.

For Phoebe, her present at first appeared to make no sense. At least not to John who was not completely aware of the girl's love of gymnastics and ribbon dancing. The first element was a brand new set of real Japanese silk ribbons which were far shorter but wider and decorated with a swirling pattern of glorious red roses which surrounded a finely embroidered turtle, for the simple reason that Phoebe adored turtles and had done so from a very early age. The second part, which she had accidentally opened first but it didn't really matter, was a very short black kimono which actually transpired to be based off the ones which one of the female dance troupes who worked with the agency used. Unlike the ones that those girls used though, this kimono was once again real silk with silver lining all around the edges and fine details in different shades of grey and gold to give it a truly unique appearance. "I checked with some of the girls who do a similar dance style to what you do Phoebe and it'll be perfectly fine for you to wear for a performance." Vincent had grinned when she saw it. "Plus, it'll really make you stand out as The Moon Princess which I am totally ditching any shows they try to put me in for to see."

Sharing a glance, both twins suddenly pounced to hug the other for entirely different reasons. Phoebe couldn't believe the fact that not only had her brother given her something so heartfelt and beautiful but he had also made a promise which normally he would never be able to keep. John hugged his brother out of nothing more than sheer pride and hoped against all hope that when he got back to his reality that Vincent would do something like this for one of them. He still remembered the spirits words, this was only a temporary transition between worlds and for a moment he wondered if it would be possible to bring Phoebe to his for a short time as well.

Now that would be a wish and a half and he wasn't sure if two could be granted in the same way. Though now he thought back, the girl had never actually said what her wish had been. Yes there was something to do with him, that much had been made clear, but what if there was a chance that she wanted to meet their absent father? Mentally he stored that away as yet another question to ask when the situation was right, it certainly would prove to be an entertaining time indeed.

Chapter 11

Little Butterfly

The sun had long ago since set but not a single one of the Henderson family felt inclined to go to sleep just yet. The night was still young and there was plenty to keep them going throughout the evening, especially now that most of the posh guests who had been invited purely out of courtesy had politely left for some other function or to deal with their cat or some other excuse. Miss Penny's status was still one that was questioned by a few who honestly believed that her fame and fortune would fade as she got older but anyone with half an eye could tell that the girl could act. So once the dainty cakes, extremely fiddly and flaky puddings had been put away and the bubbly tucked back into the cellar to keep it nice and cool, things became a much more normalised form of an extended family life.

Away from the glitz and the glamour, Penny was very much an ordinary nineteen-year-old with lots of interests to keep her amused. She was about to head off to the US to study at Julliard for a couple of years just to get the qualifications that she clearly didn't need to get though had thankfully been able to nab the boy of her dreams before any bright spark at the infamous school for acting, dance and drama could get a chance to. This had shortly been confirmed after the guests had gone when Scott had quite literally scooped the girl up into a big swinging hug before planting possibly one of the biggest kisses on her lips that anyone could imagine.

Of course there had been a massive stir over this and the pair had jokingly not been allowed to be next to each other for the rest of the night until bedtime and even then it was under threat of any noises being heard then it would be the bucket of ice cold water. To calm everyone down, Penny had wisely suggested that they order pizza, chicken and chips from a local takeaway and spend the night playing on the games console. This had been well received as a very good idea and it wasn't long before there was a heated competition going on between Lucy, Scott, Penny and Vincent as they raced around crazy tracks, picking up power ups and generally causing problems wherever they went.

Alan was watching with rapt attention, despite the fact that it was well past his bed time the youngster was still up and had previously been bouncing around the room like a mad thing after being permitted to drink cola. Any amount of sugary drinks were bound to set Alan off, and cola was the worst, but they were here to have fun at the end of the day and that was the best thing. The twins were sitting on one of the many sofas, enjoying the mad antics of the others but not joining in just yet. Both felt exhausted and tired but weren't going to lose a minute of time to not be with their whole family. Well not in entirety but that was an issue for later.

John twisted his head to the side when he realised that Phoebe was lightly clasping his hand and staring vacantly off into the distance. There was a glassy look to her eyes, almost as if something were upsetting her though there wasn't much that he could think of to say. He held the same fear in his heart at the moment, that soon the clock would strike midnight and everything would be changed back. He wasn't the type to believe in fairy story things like that but he supposed he could understand where her thoughts came from.

Lightly he tugged her arm towards himself, causing the white haired girl to blink in surprise and turn to him with a confused expression. John tugged again and eventually the girl clicked to what he wanted her to do. Slowly and carefully, almost as if she were afraid that everything was about to break and smash into a million separate pieces; Phoebe gently laid against her twin and allowed him to embrace her without a word. "Tonight," he whispered quietly. "We'll tell each other everything tonight, okay? Don't get sad, not in front of them. It's not fair."

"I know," Phoebe said with a sigh, watching as they went hell for leather trying to outdo each other on the game, "but for once I would like to just be selfish and not have to consider the thoughts of others."

John didn't reply, running his hand through the girl's hair gently and calmly. He understood her fears on an instinctual level but didn't want to betray anything to the happy faces he could see now. He watched his mother, so full of energy and love and found himself feeling highly guilty for not having focused on her. She had been the one that he wanted to see the most and that was what his wish was all about in the first place but instead he had found himself focusing more and more on his twin. Then he remembered that life had always been like that with them, they loved each other and all of that but to an outsider they would appear distant and unsure.

That was due mainly to the fact that they were both confidants for one another, the extra pillar of support that was needed to keep this mad family under control. He smiled lightly and realised that the one thing he had been missing these last five years was a sense that he was now alone and didn't have anyone to support him which was wrong. He had Scott to rely on, his father was always there and if he ever wanted to talk to Granda Micha then the phone was always waiting to be answered. He had been selfish himself, bottling up his emotions and cutting himself off from his caring family when he should have been more involved with them. "We all are selfish at times Phoebe, but very few people begrudge the like of us doing so. Let's just have some fun for now, okay?"

"Can I try to beat you at the dance game?" her words were laced with mischief and also a little bit of challenge that he hadn't quite heard before.

"Let's try and get a twin score huh?" John asked quietly, tickling Phoebe in a spot which he knew would get a response from the girl no matter what mood she was in. Letting out a peal of laughter, the girl immediately tickled him back and they went tumbling onto the floor much to the panic of everyone else.

"Whoa, what are you two doing?" Lucy said, fretting and trying to pull the pair back up together in order to hug them. "You gave me the fright of my life."

Neither twin responded, instead wrapping themselves around the form of the woman who had bared them. There were still questions to be asked and answered of course but that would be saved for another time. Lucy returned the hugs with a bemused expression but then chuckled up-roaring. "Honestly, I don't think I'll ever be able to understand the pair of you."

"We want a go on the dance game!" Phoebe said brightly, disentangling herself from the glorious smells of a mixture of perfume.

Vincent looked up with a frown. "Why? I thought you liked carting?"

"We do," John said, still holding onto his mum by the waist whilst he let Phoebe sort out the game. "But I've got a month's supply of chocolate resting on beating her at the dance challenges."

Scott was the first to let out a laugh at the very thought. "Oh, John, you should know better than to do such a thing. She'll beat you without even trying in the slightest."

Flopping onto the sofa, Vincent groaned a little as Alan took the opportunity to leap onto his stomach. "Yeah, come on, John, she can beat me without even trying and I'm getting every dance lesson under the sun at the moment." He was playfully wrestling with Alan to get the youngster off of him but the child was distracted by the bright sounds of the music game starting.

After doing a couple of practice songs to warm up, the twins went into battle mode over three songs. Not quite believing how good he felt right at this moment in time, John started not only dancing along with the last tune but also singing it as well. He wasn't the world's best singer and never would be but he didn't care in the slightest.

Slowly the final scores fell into place and there was a mixture of yells of laughter, joy and absolute disbelief. They had done as

John had said they would, they were matched evenly in all but one spot and had gotten the same rank of A Class. "No way," Vincent said, grabbing the controller to see if it were rigged. "That's just too freaky to be true!"

"Power of being twins," Phoebe said with a grin, hugging John lightly. "You should try it sometime, Vincent, it's rather fun."

Scott choked on his drink but didn't make any other additional comments and John just laughed at his misfortune. Not to be outdone in the dancing stakes, Vincent stood up and playfully pushed his brother back to the sofa to be tackled by Alan. "Well we'll see who's the best dancer out of us two. You win I get you those magazines you wanted, I win and you're coming to perform at that concert young lady!"

"Yeah, yeah," Phoebe said, flicking her white hair over her shoulder. "I'm sure your adoring Japanese fans would love the fact that your elder sister was dancing with you. There would be a riot. Still going to beat you though."

Scott plopped down next to John to pull him into an odd shaped hug as clearly Alan was about to fall asleep for the night. "Do those two ever give up?"

"Nope," John replied, leaning against his brothers, "they're both just as stubborn as Dad." For a second he saw the hurt in Scott's eyes but the other relaxed after a few seconds before leaning close. "Fancy trying to distract Vincent so Phoebe will win?"

Nodding in response, the pair readied themselves to cause trouble. The game was on and there was only going to be one winner by their standards.

Chapter 12

Whispers in the hours before dawn

Finding that for the first time in years he had been able to drift off into a very happy and pleasant sleep, John mildly groaned when he gradually became aware of something very gently shaking him. Rolling onto his back, the boy rubbed his eyes a few times and blinked to get his hazy vision into focus. "Phoebe?" he asked a few moments later, taking slightly longer than what anyone would normally have expected for someone to recognise another. It wasn't his fault that his night vision was pretty screwed up; it was just one of the many problems of being born with albinism. "What's the matter?" the girl looked paler than usual, more strained as if she were terribly worried about something.

For a while she didn't reply, instead looking away so that her hair was caught in the light from the strange night shade which they had still. It cast strange but welcoming shadows around the room and seemed to highlight the whiteness of the girl's hair, making it shimmer and shine. Vaguely John recalled the spirit who appeared to talk to him only the night before and wondered if he really had been imagining that or if he had been seeing his twin for the first time. Finally a sigh escaped Phoebe's lips, long and slow, as if she were trying to hold back tears. "I don't want to lose you, John, I don't want this to end."

Sitting up, John frowned and reached to place a hand on her head. "We both know that this is just a temporary thing, something that can only be true for a short while. The spirit said so... but you might just be getting worked up over nothing. It didn't say how long temporary would be..."

"One day and one hour exactly," Phoebe said quietly, still not looking at her twin in the slightest. "That's how long he said to me because the powers needed were so great. I never thought that it would truly happen and now..."

Pulling Phoebe into a hug, John sighed and held her there though no more words could come to him. He wanted to give her some hope; something to cling onto but there was nothing that came to mind. One day and one hour, it was an incredibly short time and possibly one of the worst things that he had ever had to consider. But then he remembered that sometimes things had to happen in only a short space of time because if they dragged out frictions could occur. Families were unpredictable things after all and if something horrible were to happen then being able to know that it was only temporary... Abruptly stopping that train of thought, the blond-haired boy shook his head and sighed. "Maybe you're taking things too literally," he said quietly, which caused the girl to look up at him with questioning eyes.

"I mean, yes it is a short time to be together but it may just have been what could be afforded." Continuing, he tried to best think of a way to explain things. "I mean, until a few hours ago I was never even aware that I was a twin though I always felt that there should be someone on the right hand side of me whenever I hugged up to Dad. Maybe we've only been given the twenty-five hours because in my world that's how long we were together."

Phoebe blinked in surprise at John. "They never told you about me?"

Shaking his head in response, the boy sighed. "No, I don't even think Scott knew because he once asked Dad about the scar on my side. I think they didn't want to talk about it because it used to make Mum really upset and she would hide away for hours upon hours. I was just too young to understand really."

"Why wouldn't Mum tell you about us?" Phoebe asked after a moment's consideration. "She told me when I was old enough to understand. Okay, granted it was when I was ten or so but surely she should have explained it to you."

Biting back the urge to cry, as well as the bile that crept up into his throat John shook his head, "Mum died when I was nine, she got involved in a car crash on the way to hospital to have Alan and didn't even survive long enough to hold him."

Staring up at her brother in shock, Phoebe tried to think how horrible it must have been but then remembered that she shared a similar pain. But clearly John had no idea about that incident and she didn't feel quite inclined to share it with him yet. Instead she wrapped herself tightly around his frame, holding him quietly and glad to be able to share these sorts of feelings with someone else for once. Yes there were all her other brothers whom she could rely on but it wasn't quite the same as being able to just be on the exact same wavelength like this.

For how long the pair were embraced it was hard to say, there was no ticking clocks in the room and the old grandfather clock downstairs never chimed out no matter what was done to try and fix it. Blinking his eyes rapidly some time later, John carefully glanced around the room and found himself still holding onto Phoebe though the girl was peacefully slumbering next to him. She looked more like a china doll than ever but he smiled and gently ran his fingers down the side of her face with a smile.

Her blue eyes snapped open and she blinked rapidly at him, mimicking his movements almost perfectly which was still slightly un-nerving. "What time is it?" she asked, blearily rubbing one hand across her eyes.

"I've no idea," John said in reply. "It's not dawn yet so we've still got plenty of time to talk if you wish to do so."

"I can't think of anything more to talk about," Phoebe said. "At least nothing that is a pleasant subject."

Wriggling a finger in his ear, a habit of when he was thinking, John pondered for a reasonable topic of conversation and then fell on one which would probably bring about some bad memories but should clear up some issues he was having of his own. "Well, one thing you can tell me about which shouldn't prove to be too much of an upsetting thing for you," he started with a smile and just a little bit of cheek in his tone. "If we were originally conjoined twins how come you're a girl and I'm a boy? There should be no possible way of such a thing happening."

It was a reasonably good question to talk about throughout the long hours before dawn he reasoned, clearly Phoebe had a good idea about what had gone on in the first few hours of life and he wanted to share in that knowledge. For a few moments

Phoebe was quiet, thinking through the best way to explain things before clicking her tongue slightly. "I'm not quite sure to be strictly honest; all I know is that on the original birth certificate that was issued for us we were recorded as Phoebe and Jane Henderson."

John's eyes rose comically wide. "Jane?"

"Yes, Jane." The girl looked a bit uncomfortable. "When I asked Mum about it she said that I had a twin sister who was joined to me but she died a couple of hours after the procedure."

It was John's turn to be quiet for a few long seconds. Apparently in this world he had been a girl which made no real sense because he was sure that he had been born a boy. Unless in his world the other baby had been a boy as well but somehow that didn't add up in his mind. Sure there were going to be differences but conjoined twins like them definitely did not happen. Slowly he blinked, remembering something from a very strange and rather horrifying sex education lesson he had gone through once.

He couldn't remember the name of the syndrome but apparently there were cases where a baby could be born one sex and then change due to an imbalance or a sudden surge from the distinctive Y-chromosome which was present in all males. He couldn't say for certain if that applied to him or not but he made a mental note to try and find the original and the re-issued birth certificates back home to check his theory out. "You know what?" he said to make up for his silence. "I don't think it really matters. We've got each other and right now that's more than enough for me."

Phoebe grinned. "I agree. We should make tomorrow morning really special, something to store in our memory banks forever."

"What if we forget everything though?" The thought had suddenly popped into the male twins head and he didn't know rightly what to think of such an idea. "Once the time is up and we go back to normal. What if it never happened?"

"We write it down." The reply was immediate and slightly unexpected. "I'm sure there's got to be some forgotten notebooks lying around somewhere. All we have to do is write in them as much as we possibly can and then hide them… that way if we do forget everything we can find them at a later date and ponder them for hours upon hours."

John smiled and nodded. "That sounds a grand plan, twinny."

Chapter 13

Home

Almost not wishing to open his eyes when the door was lightly rapped on by Paul only a few mere hours after the secret talk, John blinked blearily at the clock and groaned. "Do I have to get up?"

"If you want to be able to have some breakfast before Vincent and his cohorts manage to eat us out of house and home I would recommend it, sir," Paul said with a polite tone and accent which he recognised all too well as disguising a laug., "Though I must say that your sister is giving them a fair run for their money."

Suddenly sitting upright, John realised that Phoebe had not only obviously gotten up and sorted everything out but had even packed their few things into plastic bags. He blinked and glanced again at the clock, seeing that it was only five thirty a.m. and wondering if the girl was used to being up at this time in the morning. He concluded that it was more than likely given the fact that she was a dancer and more than likely couldn't stay out too late during the summer months. Hastily he pulled himself upright and got sorted out with washing, brushing his teeth and getting dressed. As he went to rush downstairs, a small leather bound note book slipped off the bed where Phoebe had been and clattered to the floor.

Gathering it up, he frowned lightly at the book for a few seconds before remembering that he was supposed to write everything down for Phoebe but would probably have to wait until he was in the car. For a second he thought that this might be the book that she had done for him but upon seeing the word 'diary' written in faded golden letters he thought it best to put it back where he had found it.

"John!" Scott's voice cut immediately through his hearing, nearly startling him as his black haired brother glared at him through the door. "Are you ever going to come down for breakfast or am I going to have to drag you down?"

Managing to look suitably flustered, John grimaced at his brother and nodded. "I'm coming, just slept in a bit was all."

Scott rolled his eyes and carefully grabbed his brother's arm, before purposefully dragging the other down the stairs. "Overslept? You were supposed to be up at five, not five thirty. Come on, we're going to hit traffic if we're not careful."

It was some time after nine in the morning that the family was eventually able to get away from Penny's house because Vincent unfortunately had to cut his time short with his family due to some photo shoot which had finally been arranged at the last minute. It was clear that the young boy wasn't happy about it in the slightest but promised a million times over that he would ensure to get some proper time off soon and come and visit them. There had been many hugs, lots of heartfelt words and an air of general despondency about the whole situation.

Sharing a glance when it was their turn to say goodbye to Vincent, the twins scooped him up into a joint hug and squished him tightly like they used to do when the other was small. Phoebe placed an overly large and definitely faked smooch on his cheek whilst John quite gladly ruffled his hair until it was a complete and total mess. "Hoi! Mum! Get them off me!"

"Nope," said Phoebe, holding onto him all the tighter, "you're not going; you're staying here with us forever and ever."

"That's right," John said, "we'll lock you in the biggest cupboard we can find and throw away the key and everything."

"You two are morons!" Vincent said, managing to deftly wiggle out of their grips but chuckling at them good naturedly. He sometimes thought that he always missed the twins the most because they were constants in his lives. They didn't change personality much; they had known what they were going to be from an early age and stuck to it. He wasn't to know that before the day was out, he would only be aware of one twin in his life but which one that would be was yet to say. "But I love you for it. I'll e-mail the pair of you when I get to a computer, if the filters aren't completely and totally nuts that is… all right, I'm coming!" Turning, the boy ran towards his Japanese stage director who was yelling furiously at him to hurry up and get a move on.

The family stood side by side, all waving to the disappearing cars and vans and offering comfort to Lucy who despite the years upon years of having her son being big in the music world somewhere far away from home, still cared for him. In fact she cared for all of her children so much and would have loved to keep them all at home but it was an impossible thing. Children could not be wrapped in plastic forever, they had to fly the nest and face the big wide world someday. John cast a long glance at his mother before wrapping his arms protectively around her neck, as he was just an inch or two bigger than her now and could easily do so these days. Lightly he let his senses take in every last detail of the woman he was about to lose for a second time in his life.

John tried to commit to memory the fell of her thick, golden hair, the softness of her dark tanned skin, the way her breath tickled his nose when she would laugh and the dazzling smile that would be sent his way whenever the woman spotted her child. He didn't want to leave this feeling, didn't want to go back to a world where she was no longer there but there was only so much magic in the world. If indeed it was magic that had caused this and it wasn't all some very realistic feeling dream. That would just be the worst if he were to open his eyes and find himself back at the caravan with everything just the same as it normally was. He would feel a fool and completely cheated on everything which would only serve to put him in a bad mood that was not a good thing.

"I'm all right now," Lucy said lightly, patting his hands affectionately, "thank you, John."

For a second he didn't want to let go, even though he knew that time was running short, but slowly he released his hand and smiled at his mother. Another hand took his and he stared once again at the matching eyes of Phoebe and knew she understood him far better than anyone else in this situation right now. "Cheer up, he'll be back for Christmas or the very latest our next birthday," she said gently, trying to cover the truth of her words.

"I think he just likes getting to confuse his fans with pictures of us two but I could be wrong."

Chuckling, John tugged Phoebe into a very brief hug that would pass the attention and notice of the rest of the family. Alan was too young to understand anything and was already in a mood because he had been woken up far too early in the morning when he didn't need to be which was just the worst thing for a little six-year-old boy. Scott was talking to Penny, though his lips were firmly locked on hers and likewise were the young ladies locked on his. Lucy was trying to get Paul to stop putting things into the van but was interrupted by a phone call from Granda Micha asking if she wanted him to bring the dogs straight back home or could he keep them for the weekend.

The twins knew that this was their goodbye but neither wanted to say those words. "Come on," John said at length. "Let's go and help Mum out, huh?"

Once the cars were loaded and the final goodbyes said, the family clambered into the car that they had arrived in and headed for the one place that they all could agree on was one of the best in the world, home. Lucy put some stories on the CD player to keep Alan entertained whilst Scott lounged in the boot of the small people carrier and tried to deal with his horrendous aversion to car-sickness. The twins were far more subdued than anyone in the car could normally remember them to be but small details were fading though it was barely noticeable at first. Becoming aware that he was nodding off to sleep, which was virtually unheard of for the pale skinned boy, John tried to focus on the current story to keep himself awake but found that it just didn't work which was odd. The car seemed to slow down, like it was weighted down with something or made out of lead. His head lolled forward and faintly he felt Phoebe's hand reach out and tug him onto her lap.

Forcing his eyes open, he stared up at his twin and was shocked to see that she was fading. No, fading wasn't the right word for it, it was more like she was dissolving away but it looked like pure specks of white light were just gently floating away from the source that they had gathered around. Soon all he could see was Phoebe's glowing eyes as the white particles increased in number, "I'm always with you, John, never forget that." Her final words were whispered and then there was a final flourish and all the particles were gone. John's eyes snapped closed and he lay still for some time, but for a moment just before a deep slumber took him, words gently escaped his lips, "I'll miss you, Phoebe."

~

Snapping open his eyes, John sat upright and stared incomprehensibly around the room before recognising it as his own. It was basic by most boys' standards, with light blue walls and a deep blue carpet mainly covered by furniture. The ceiling was a light shade of grey with careful replications of star charts which he and his father had done last year with help from Scott. The desk was messy, despite the fact that the computer and most of the files needed to be put into the cardboard boxes for going to the states to study. Feeling as if something was missing, John carefully got out of bed and walked to the window, opening the blinds and staring out at the rolling fields and the small hamlet village which appeared perfectly normal and as it should be.

Shaking his head, the boy rubbed his eyes and nearly jumped when the door opened. "Oh, sorry, didn't realise you were up son," Jeff smiled at him with a chuckle. "I was just coming up to check on you."

With no real inclination as to why, John suddenly found himself wrapped around his father tightly and holding onto him as if his life depended on it. Tears stung his eyes though he couldn't recall why. Jeff smiled, holding John close and gently running a hand through his son's hair. "Oh my, John, it's all been a bit much for you hasn't it?"

"What has?" John finally managed to be able to blurt out; finding his throat hurt and the tears were still running in rivets down his face.

Leading his son back to his bed, Jeff sighed lightly and ran a hand through his black hair. His age was showing ever so slightly these days, John noted, there were many grey streaks coming through and definitely a selection of lines running down his face which he was sure hadn't been there before. "This whole bloody week, I thought I'd have known better than to let anyone go near that box but you know what Alan's like," Jeff looked guilty though John couldn't think of a reason why he would be so. "I really thought that we had lost you for a while, John, you scared me."

Frowning, John suddenly found his memory working overtime as if it were just realising there was a big gap. They had gone on holiday to see Penny, Vincent had turned up unexpectedly and then had to go again but had arranged some time off from his hectic schedule. When they had got home, Scott had helped him to start packing up for going aboard and sorting through the mounds of things that he had when suddenly there had been a crash upstairs. Rushing up, they had found Alan in amongst the remains of a dark wooden box which had been their mothers and a whole host of different papers had been scattered.

Gathering them up, John had found what appeared to be a birth certificate and reading it he had realised two things with a harsh horror. The first was that he had been born a twin and the second was that according to the certificate, he had also been a Jane. The rest was hazy but he remembered vaguely about the doctor visiting him, words of advice being given to Jeff and then just a calm blackness. "I'm sorry," John said at length, shaking his head. "I shouldn't have reacted like that."

Hugging his son tightly, Jeff smiled. "Hey I would have probably done the same to be honest. At least you're awake now which is what I've been waiting for. Scott will be pleased, he hasn't been off the phone…" Almost on cue there came a sharp ring and the father rolled his eyes skywards. "Speak of the devil and he shall appear. I'll go and get him before he flies into frenzy on the answer phone again, you can talk to him if you like."

Without waiting for the nod which he knew would be answering him, Jeff stood up and headed to go and answer the phone. For a few moments John sat where he was; a deep frown upon his face before quite suddenly he stood up and walked towards his desk. Fiddling on with a catch which released a secret compartment, he eventually managed to get his fingers around the complicated mechanism and pulled it open. In all the years he had had the desk he had never once hidden anything in the secret compartment, there was never any point to do so because it was that complicated to get into.

But this time there was something. It was a small, flat book bound in brown leather. Lightly he picked it up and just faintly managed to read the words 'diary' written in gold text. It appeared that the book had been dropped in a puddle of water or something but had been carefully dried out at some point in time before being placed in the desk.

Carefully he opened the book and managed to read the name 'Phoebe Henderson' before Jeff was back in the room with a frantic Scott on the phone. Pushing the drawer closed, John took the phone and decided to deal with the mysterious book later on. It would probably make good reading when he was travelling to the other side of the world.

He had no recollection of the events which had taken place with his twin sister and none what so ever of the wish he had made in order to see his mother. He didn't even notice that high above his computer desk, in a silver gilded frame was a photograph of a young woman with a two-year-old baby girl smiling joyfully at the camera. John always thought that it showed some distant cousin or else was just a random photograph that had found its way into the family collection. He was completely unaware that it was the last photograph which had been taken of his mother Lucy and her one and only daughter before the little girl had gone into a sleep that she would never wake from.

None of the boys had been told about little Phoebe, and she was never mentioned to John because no one was sure how he would take it. The little girl should not have lived past the first few days of her life but made it to at least her second birthday. Without her twin by her side.

Life sometimes can be cruel, but that is just the way of things. Little sparks of light always remain though and somewhere, someone always remembers the truth and simple love that cannot ever be unbroken.

Part II

The Brother I Never Had

Chapter 1

Candles

Having closed the door firmly five minutes ago, Phoebe Henderson was not surprised to hear the quiet knock on it and sighed lightly before walking over and opening it. Alan, her youngest brother looked sheepishly at her and extended his arms upwards. Somehow the youngster always managed to look incredibly pathetic and childlike despite the fact that he was determined to tell everyone that he was grown up already. The beauty of being eight years old was something that Phoebe sometimes missed but in other ways was glad that she was no longer burdened with such troubles. "They still arguing?" she asked, bending down to pick up the boy being careful to ensure that her skirt did not get trapped in the doorway.

For the last few years now, the girl had foregone the wearing of light-coloured clothes and was dressing in dark browns, purples, greys, blacks and other such colours but strangely she managed to pull them off. The dark colours highlighted her pale skin and the now whiteness of her hair, which was another surge of her continual suffering of Albinism which had plagued her since her birth nearly eighteen years ago. Not that she minded it was something which made her unique in her family and that was the way she liked things to be. Granted it could be a bit of a pain but there was little that could honestly be done about it, so instead of wallowing in self-pity, she made up for it by making her difference part of her beauty.

At least that was how Granda Micha had told her to use it, when she had tried to return her grandmother's green dress to him after a visit to the caravan. He had refused, saying that she looked simply wonderful in it and should use it as a starting point for becoming her own stylish person. What the old man quite thought of the dark look was yet unknown but somehow Phoebe knew that he wouldn't mind. He had always said that there was a great bit of his Hannah in the girl and she would have probably still been wearing the outrageous clothes that she wore if she were alive. But those thoughts were only subjectively on her mind. Right now there was a much bigger problem in the house and really the girl wished that it was all over.

There was an argument going on downstairs, but not the usual kind of argument. Living in a house with one younger brother could be tiresome at times but Phoebe knew that it was just due to the rather large age gap between them and the youngster not quite understanding that no meant no when it came to playing constantly all the time. Scott, her eldest brother had left to go and join the RAF as well as start up a proper home with his beloved Penelope who he was planning to marry the next year so when he came back things were usually highly fun and definitely the type of thing that made everyone happy.

Her only other brother, a mischievous and very handsome young man who was generally considered to be the spitting image of their father who had sadly passed away not seven months ago, was generally not seen around the house because he had a record contract in Japan and a whole host of adoring fans. Vincent had secretly confided in Phoebe that sometimes he preferred being at home where the only people who really knew him where his family and friends from childhood. When the other was home, Phoebe had to usually be very quick in hiding all reference to her obsession with Japanese music because the group she hung out with at college were all into it.

Not that Vincent would have probably minded, but there was still just a niggling doubt in the back of the girl's mind that the idea of your sister sitting listening to your music and having fantasy's about the guys that you sung with would be rather difficult. The only other person in permanent residence in the house these days, other than the two Springer Spaniels Amberly and Diesel, was their mother Lucy who was a woman on a mission. Having finally been able to let go of all the years of pent up sadness with the passing of the only man she had ever truly loved, the woman had grieved properly for the first time in a long while and decided that she was going to pursue her career to the full extent.

Of course she still missed her darling Jeff like any doting wife should do but the time was ripe to move on and she had done so. There was no mention of anyone being possibly on the horizon but none of the older children were going to begrudge their mother another shot at happiness if someone eventually came along.

Knowing right now that Alan wasn't in the middle of any arguments with her Mum, Phoebe rolled her eyes and sighed. Clearly their bossy Grandmother was the culprit this time and who knew what the old bat was arguing about now. Thankfully she wasn't in the house, so the argument was taking place over the phone but Phoebe was used to this sort of thing occurring. Grandmother Christina was from Jeff's side of the family and had always been of the opinion that her son had married well below his worth. On numerous occasions she had tried to split the pair up and even once accused Lucy of abandoning her, at the time, only son Scott but thankfully they had cleared that one up.

Christina was the type of woman who would not let anything lye once she had it firmly stuck in her head and was pretty much a stubborn woman to shift. Sometimes Phoebe wished that Grandma Hannah was around because she was sure that the old Jamaican woman with the fair skin could have pounded Grandmother Christina into the floor without even laying a punch on her. "Why are they arguing?" Alan asked, looking up to his sister with large eyes.

Phoebe shrugged her shoulders, "Who knows, Alan, sometimes I wish that old bag would leave us all alone… actually it's probably something to do with me."

"About that course you're going to take…" the young boy asked, swinging his legs back and forth on the bed whilst he looked around his sister's room. It was tidy and pristine as it always had been but he smiled at seeing the dancing awards on her shelves, the turtle figurines which she had collected since she was a child and the photographs which jostled for place on the bookcase with the collection of books that the girl had gotten over the years. "Why should she be worried about that? Mum was over the moon when you got accepted," he continued, moving towards the photographs whilst his sister was fiddling about with something on one of her two desks, "I can't see what's wrong with a girl going off to a dancing school."

Chuckling, Phoebe didn't look up from her complicated work. "Oh don't worry about her, Alan, I'm sure that everything will be sorted out soon. Mum knows how to deal with her now."

Alan didn't question what his sister was doing on her desk, though he was curious as he could see a selection of candles and ribbon. He knew that his sister was sensible and direct but at times she could have her flights of fantasy. Then his eyes fell upon her calendar and just faintly he could make out the words 'Tony, Candle shoot' in the box for October 30th. He chuckled. "You have told Mum that Tony's coming over haven't you? She wasn't too happy last time he did."

Phoebe grimaced a little at that thought but nodded. "Yeah she knows and last time it was a misunderstanding, pure and simple." Tony was one of Phoebe's best friends in the world and he liked to use her as a model for his clothing range. He was heavily into the Gothic Lolita fashion and had a rather tidy little business going on the internet at the moment and was looking to start up his own shop in London which would be good for the pair of them as it meant they could rent a flat together. The only slightly worrisome thing was that Tony was completely oblivious to the fact that Phoebe had rather more than a crush on him but was too shy to admit anything about her feelings. The last time he had come to do a photo shoot with Phoebe, the outfit she was modelling for him was perfectly innocent as it was a sort of gothic fairy but unfortunately just at the second that Lucy had walked into the room with milk and cookies for the pair Tony had been trying to fix part of the sleeve which had just ripped unexpectedly and it had looked like something else altogether.

Thankfully it had all been cleared up but the literal outcry from Lucy had been enough to nearly cause an international scandal. Actually Tony had craftily used the pictures as part of a competition he was in and they helped him to get fourth place overall which was great for someone of his standing. "Are you ever going to tell him?" Alan asked before receiving a clip around the head from his sister who half glared at him.

"I thought you came in here to escape the argument, not go on at me about that sort of thing," she said, with a sigh, but passed it off as nothing other than a tease from her brother who just smiled cheekily and looked up once again at her photograph collection. Suddenly he spotted a silver gilded one which he had not seen before. It showed a young looking woman holding onto a very small baby who was wrapped in a blue blanket. "Hey, I've not seen that one before. Is it new?"

Phoebe turned away from her work and looked towards the photo the youngster had pointed out. She felt a stab of pain go through her heart and lightly turned her head away, "Not quite, it's one that I found a while ago but didn't display it properly until a couple of years ago. Don't know quite why."

Sensibly Alan decided to drop the subject because he could see that whatever it was clearly upset his sister. Tilting his head to the side, the eight-year-old listened for a few seconds and grinned. "I think they've stopped arguing. I'm going to check how Mum is and then see if I can help her with the Halloween decorations for tomorrow."

"All right, I'll be down soon," Phoebe said, smiling as she watched Alan open her door and go running down the stairs. Lightly she sighed, letting out a breath through her nose and glancing back at the picture. "It's a good thing that I don't have to explain everything to him these days, isn't it, Jane?" she asked quietly before looking out of her window to see the rain starting to set in. "Oh well, I guess I will need that parasol, though I do hate using that thing."

Jane wasn't an imaginary friend; she was the other girl who should have been in Phoebe's life. What the seventeen-year-old didn't know, however, or remember for that fact was that not two years ago she had met the person she called Jane. But they had been called John, her twin brother who had been separated from her as they had been originally joined together. Of course he had originally been the Jane which Phoebe still talked to whenever she was completely alone and they were still connected but neither one really remembered anything about the other.

Sighing, she shook her head as her mobile started to ring and picked it up with a smile. Tony was calling to check that everything was going to be all right for tonight and she got the impression that there was just a little more to his visit than the usual high jinks that he liked to play. Replying to the text message quickly, she rose with the idea of going downstairs to help her Mum with carving the pumpkins for a while but then was struck by a sudden impulse. Carefully rummaging around in the drawers of her desk, Phoebe pulled out a special little candle holder which she had had as long as she could remember. It was in the shape of two birds though the artwork had faded over the years so that it was impossible to tell what they had originally been.

Taking hold of her metal night light, which was shaped like the old fashioned lamps with stars in the top to allow the air in and the heat out safely, the girl placed the smaller holder in the chamber and carefully placed a thin, silvery white candle in it. Using a taper to light it, Phoebe safely closed the door and moved the lantern to the windowsill which was always kept free of objects for this very reason. Carefully she moved the net curtains out of harm's way and placed the lantern dead centre. "There you go, little spirit, a light to bring you home." She smiled before glancing at the dreary weather and smiling. She preferred it when it was overcast; it meant that she didn't have to cover up as much.

Turning away, the girl headed downstairs to go and help her mother out and wait for Tony to arrive. She didn't see that just for a moment, the candle glowed a little brighter and a small white particular danced on an unseen breeze before landing lightly on the strange lamp which Vincent had bought her two years before.

Chapter 2

Pumpkins

If there was one thing in the entire world that Lucy Henderson could genuinely claim to be absolutely useless at, Halloween pumpkins was definitely that. No matter how many times the middle aged woman with the blonde hair tried, she could always somehow end up in the situation where there would be more mess than actual pumpkin left. How, a total mystery but thankfully this year, Phoebe was had managed to get hold of the three pumpkins and order her mother firmly to sit at the table and watch instead of fussing. To appease the woman, she had promised that she would save the insides and her mother could spend hours upon hours making all the pies, cakes and soups that she wanted afterwards.

Lucy sighed and shook her head. "What I would do without you around, my dear little Phoebe, I do not know."

"Probably end up buying plastic pumpkins like every other mum on the street and just fetch them out of the attic every other year," Phoebe replied without taking her eyes off her careful work of cutting a reasonable size hole in the top of the largest pumpkin.

Smiling, Lucy regarded her daughter for a few long moments and reflected on just how lucky she had been. Yes there were many tragedies in her life but there was many in every life because that was just the way that things went. Life and death had to be balanced but she very much doubted that there were many Phoebe's in the world. Her one and only daughter was her life-force, one of the many things that kept her tethered to reality and she could not wait until the day when the young lady blossomed into a fully-fledged woman. She got the impression that maybe such things weren't as far off as she imagined but since both parties were about as clueless as each other in regards to that little circumstance, the sensible non-Jamaican side of her told her to leave well enough alone.

Not that Lucy actually bothered to listen to that side of her personality much; it was the dull boring and official part of herself who got firmly left at work the second five thirty one rolled around. Sometimes she felt guilty for having to work quite late but the kids managed perfectly fine so she wasn't worried. Phoebe removed the top off the pumpkin and began scooping out large chunks of pumpkin mush into one of several large bowls which were neatly lined up on the bench. Lucy had to wonder where the girl got her organisation abilities from because they definitely weren't a trait of hers and certainly did not belong to Jeff but that was by the by. They could have come from Granda Micha of course; he was always so neat and tidy so it had probably skipped a generation or two with her.

"Have you decided if you're going to that dance tomorrow night yet?" Lucy asked with a grin, knowing fine well that her daughter wouldn't have even considered it yet.

For a few seconds Phoebe was quiet, concentrating on her task of digging out the last bits of mulch from the bottom of the pumpkin. Her mother noted that she wasn't bothering to keep her dark pinafore style dress very clean but then remembered about the visitor tonight, "I'm sure he would go with you if you were to ask."

"Mother," Phoebe said, using the term to indicate that she did not want to talk about the subject any further.

Lucy just chuckled. "Oh come on, sweetheart, you know fine well that I know you want to go to that ball with that young gentleman and I'm giving you every last permission to go," she sighed, shaking her head, "you really can't let that beautiful dress go to waste can you?"

Pausing in her task of drawing lines onto the outer part of the orange object in front of her, Phoebe sighed and looked down. Her white hair slipped elegantly down, obscuring her face and it was clear why Tony liked to use her for photographs. Quite simply the girl looked so fragile and doll like that it was near impossible to tell the difference most of the time. Twirling the pen about her fingers, Phoebe sighed. "He's already going out with someone... a girl called Elizabeth."

Raising an eyebrow, Lucy shook her blonde locks at her virtually white daughter as she crept around to start braiding her long hair out of habit. If there was one thing to cheer up Phoebe it was someone gently styling her hair. "And how many photographers who have girlfriends do you know who come around to some other girl's house with clothes custom-made to fit them and take photographs?"

"I'm telling the truth, Mum, I saw him kissing her the other day," Phoebe said, beginning to draw on the rough surface once again though not with the same conviction as before, "at school in front of everyone."

Lucy sighed and was about to console her daughter when she felt the slightest vibration under her fingers and suddenly grabbed her in a rough hug. "You are a sly little devil, Phoebe Henderson, Tony wouldn't dare go out with anyone other than you and you bloody well know it girl. Sum up some courage and ask him out to that blooming dance will you? It would make everyone so happy and pleased."

Phoebe chuckled, looking up at her mum and leaning lightly back on her out of habit. She knew that the other was just being concerned and flapping on because she could see everything happening and wanted her daughter to be happy but it was just a little bit on the annoying side. Still at least she could wind her mother other up with it for a short time. Playing jokes was something that she was very good at by now. "I'll see," she said in order to placate the other, "but I'm not going to guarantee anything. You best go and stop Alan… he's just run off towards the sweet cupboard."

Turning her head roughly away, Lucy was immediately off after her youngest son with a yell that Phoebe couldn't quite make out. Shaking her head, she returned to her previous task of sorting out the pumpkins. The biggest one turned out to be the easiest to do because there was plenty of room to skilfully place the various cutting knives to turn it into a grinning menace fairly easily. Lightly the nearly eighteen-year-old began humming to herself, getting completely absorbed in her work and missing several text messages that came through. They would have only slightly irritated her anyway so it was probably for the best.

The average size pumpkin was a bit more complicated, especially when it transpired that the stork actually went further down than she had suspected it to do so. Finally though it was grinning next to its big brother and looking just as good. Vaguely she was aware of Lucy and Alan charging about, trying to get sweets off the youngster was almost as bad as trying to get a wasp off a nectar rich plant. The smallest pumpkin turned out to be one of the toughest she had ever dealt with, it was thick skinned and the pulp inside was so tightly packed that by the time she got to finally finishing getting it all out, she looked more like a pumpkin than ever before.

Rubbing her hand over her face, she sighed and glared at the smallest pumpkin on the table. "Next time I'm going with Mum to pick you, she's not pulling that one on me again."

"Oh really?" said a deep and honey-drizzled voice as a pair of hands wrapped around her middle, causing Phoebe to jump slightly before shyly half melt into the hold. "I thought that you were the expert at sorting out pumpkins?"

Lightly digging Tony in the ribs, Phoebe turned to face her friend and stuck her tongue out at him. "I am, but when they're small, tight and downright obnoxious to get around even I get the right to complain."

Grinning, Tony roughly ruffled his favourite girl's hair and chuckled at the angry glare he received back. The effect was somewhat spoilt by the fact that the girl was covered in orange seeds and pulp but he wouldn't comment on it. Not if he wanted to get his photos tonight. Tony was tall for his age, pushing on for nearly seven foot last time he had been measured and was broad shouldered with a cheeky grin and kiss curled shoulder length hair. He wasn't considered to be overly attractive; on the whole he was quite plain looking with nothing other than his height to make him distinctive. Maybe a slight dark tanning to the skin from that fact that he played rugby and basketball during the summer and the fact that his eyes were virtual deep brown pools that drew you in but other than that he was just normal looking. At least by a majority of the girls at the school they both attended.

To Phoebe though he was beautiful and when she walked next to him, she didn't feel so strange and different. Sure people still sent them funny looks but it was more because they noticed Tony's height before the relatively average and rather pale girl next to him. It was a selfish thought really but when she had told him about it the other summer he had simply laughed and said that it was one of the nicest things that anyone had ever said to him in a very long time. "Oh my little white rabbit, you are so easy to annoy. But I wouldn't have you any other way." Tony had started calling Phoebe 'white rabbit' ever since they had gotten into the Gothic Lolita business, using it as her name on his photographs so that no one would tease her at school.

Not that the girls at school actually bothered with the magazines that Tony's photo's got published in but a couple had strayed to the newspapers which caused a stir indeed. Rolling her bright blue eyes, Phoebe ran her sticky hand playfully across his nose. "For that you can finish off that pumpkin, I'm going to have a shower and get changed."

As she was heading out of the door, Tony turned briskly and caught her arm. "Ah no you don't. Sit down."

"Why?" the question covered a lot more ground than just the simple pretext as the girl was spun elegantly around before being picked up and plonked onto a clean chair, "Tony!"

"Patience, rabbit, patience," Tony said with a grin before quickly dodging around the opposite side of her and covering her eyes with his hand.

Squirming, Phoebe laughed at his antics because he could always be so random like this but in a really lovely way. "I swear if you're going to try and put any make-up on me like last time…" she said, managing to pry his fingers away from her eyes to find herself staring at a proper cup cake with all the frosting in a multi-coloured rainbow. White edible flowers decorated the edges and a single candle stood at its centre, a beautiful silvery white, with an eagle holder which completely failed to hide the gold and Sapphire ring sitting at the base of it.

Looking up to Tony with a mixture of shock, delight and awe on her face, Phoebe didn't know what to say but thankfully didn't have to. With only a slight movement their lips touched, just a light brush before becoming a small quick and delicate kiss that left her wanting more. "Will the beautiful Alice accept this Mad Hatter's invitation to the Tea Party?" His voice was a mere whisper but the girl could hear every last word. "Then to dance the night away at the court of the White Queen who she surpasses in every ounce of beauty."

Blushing pink, Phoebe nodded as her words were caught in her throat and instinctively she leaned forward to place a deeper kiss on his lips. "But how?"

"No." He placed his index finger on her lips. "Don't a say a word yet."

Turning to the cupcake, Tony lit the candle which sparkled like a firework. "Happy Unbirthday to you, my white queen, make a wish and we shall be blessed forever." His big strong arms wrapped around her frame and held her tightly for a few seconds as he felt a panic grip the girl but then a short, sharp puff of air sent the sparks flying all around the room in a dizzying display. Phoebe's blue eyes reflected them as she raised her head, following the sparks and becoming faintly aware that there seemed to be a small break in time. Even though she did not cast her eyes around the room, she was aware that everything was bathed in silver light and that Tony's warm breath had frozen in small swirls close to her ear.

Near the ceiling a figure materialised out of the joining silver particles, a small mischievous looking pixie like man with a silver tuxedo jacket and top hat. However it was clear that the man was some form of creature, a cat or something akin to a cat at the very least. "Ah, Miss Phoebe Henderson, we meet at last." The well-educated tones of a British scholar escaped the cat creature as he appeared to dance down towards the table top and land lightly on the pumpkins which she had been preparing, "you have been granted another wish since last time things went a little against your favour, not that it effected the power in the slightest of course."

"Last time?" Phoebe asked before blinking rapidly as the creature came closer to her with a great big smile on his face.

He nodded. "But no mind, you have been fortunate enough to be given another wish. You can have whatever you want for a day, what will it be, White Rabbit?"

The only wish that Phoebe could even think of right then and there didn't make much sense to the girl and later she would ponder why she had made something so silly but she knew that time was of the essence. "I wish that I could see my twin one more time."

The cat grinned before suddenly disappearing in a vivid flash which registered as that of a camera causing Phoebe to turn and almost dive towards her mother in fright and panic. Thankfully Tony still had hold of her and lightly he swung her around back onto her feet, hugging her tightly. Returning the hug, Phoebe was sure that she couldn't possibly feel any happier and put the strange vision down to nothing more than a spell of dizziness caused by sheer joy.

If she had been paying attention, she would have just faintly heard the words, "Wish most certainly granted, my dear one," but she was distracted by Tony placing the ring on her finger and swinging her around the room once more. Lucy was over the moon and fussing as she always did and Alan just couldn't see what the fuss was all about but Tony soon had him giggling away like an idiot. Phoebe smiled and got the feeling that when the clock struck midnight; things were certainly going to be magically special on the day of the souls of the dead.

Chapter 3

Trick O' Treat

"Hmm," said Tony after a moment or two, "I think that you would look good in this pattern but I don't know if I want to market it overly much or not."

Looking up from her sprawled position on the floor, in her favourite dressing gown in order to keep some decorum of modesty whilst her now boyfriend faffed over the fine details of the pictures he was going to take tonight, Phoebe looked between the three options she had. The first was a rather plain, but very well designed, black dress with white trimming and a lot of accessories to make it up into something that looked rightfully like she belonged to *The Adams Family*. The second choice was much more to her liking, a dark Victorian style dress with lace collar and a violin case which she simply adored. The main part of the dress swirled around with a dark flower print with a brown overcoat which could easily be matched with a pleasant looking umbrella, given the night's drizzle which unfortunately appeared to be setting in.

The final choice, which Phoebe had rejected on site, was a bright baby blue dress with pink frills and an assortment of white card themed accessories. Whilst she didn't mind being the dark

Alice in Wonderland she most certainly didn't want to be the simpering little child of it. But there wasn't a lot that could be said, if Tony needed to promote that style then she was his model and she would have to wear it, despite the fact that she would probably disappear under all the white. "If you don't know, why did you bring it then? I mean it's not exactly like I could pull that style off... I'll appear like the Cheshire Cat more than anything else. Turning invisible."

Tony chuckled, looking over to his white rabbit and smiling at her. "Okay, okay that helps me in that particular choice. It's just a shame it's a crummy night, the other two aren't going to show up brilliantly in this little lot."

About to query if they should go through with the photo shoot tonight, given the weather, Phoebe was surprised when Alan piped up all of a sudden as he ran past the door. "Why don't you wear that cream brown one! It'll work wonders. I'm off to the shops, see you soon!"

Looking at one another in confusion, they both asked, "What?" at the exact same moment before Phoebe sighed, "Promise not to laugh okay?"

Indicating that he wouldn't, Tony politely averted his eyes from the girl's wardrobe because he thought it would be best not to be looking in there. It was a very old fashioned habit, brought about by his Grandfather who was old fashioned in his values and who had virtually raised the boy since he was around five years old. Even he was prepared to admit that it was an odd situation but given the fact that both of his parents had run off to join the circus, quite literally in fact, things just had to be taken as they were.

"You can look now." Phoebe's voice drifted over and he turned his head to the sound of it instinctively. Lying on the bed, over the top of the other two was a lovely creamy chocolate-coloured sleeveless dress made out of a soft cashmere style material which had been trimmed back artistically. It was lined with a sweet little lace hemming and hand stitched on the front was a face of a white bear with black button eyes and nose. A plain brown shirt was worn underneath the main dress with light linen work on the collar and sleeves and the young man had a fair idea about which socks and shoes would best go with it.

The girl shuffled a bit. "It's not as good as anything you make but Granda Micha said I should try to find my own style and I gave it a go."

Picking it up carefully, Tony smiled at the simplification but the sheer splendour as well. It perfectly matched the image and in his mind's eye he knew it would work fantastically. A chuckle escaped him. "Next time I'm stuck for a choice I'm definitely going to be calling your little brother in. We'll use this and get your mum to put your hair up in bunches with matching brown ribbons. You'll look simply divine."

"But I thought you wanted to do a candle shoot with darkness and other things," Phoebe said, though she was smiling as the other gathered the other dresses up into their respective bags. It was an odd change of character for the boy whom she had known for the last eight or so years.

Tilting his head to the side, Tony winked at the other in a teasing way. "Yeah but dark things can be cute as well."

~

The rain had finally slacked off by the time that the photo shoot had been set up but thankfully the wetness of the wooden summer house gave it a bit of an extra atmosphere which was fantastic for the photos. Tony dressed the small summer house with fake cotton spider webs, the pumpkins which had been made before and even managed to eventually get a small fire going in the grate without much hassle. In his mind's eye he created the image, how he wanted everything to be and carefully arranged the furniture this way and that until he was pleased.

Lucy came wandering up first, a hairbrush in her hand and she smiled at the boy. "Well, I must admit you gave us all a bit of a surprise."

"Hello, Mrs Henderson," the boy smiled, in the process of moving a high backed wicker chair to its proper location. "I thought it best to catch Phoebe off guard."

"You certainly did that, young man." Lucy smiled back, going to help him move the chair, as despite its rather flimsy look it was in fact quite heavy due to a hidden compartment in the bottom. "Still, I'm glad you did, I was beginning to panic and think of drastic measures to get you two together."

Wincing slightly at the words, Tony didn't reply for a few moments as he dusted off the seat and then wandered over to his tripod held camera just to check that the lighting was going to be okay. Of course he would need to double check it once Phoebe was there but he liked to be at least eighty-five per cent ready before the girl turned up. "You're not going to be too fretful, are you?" he asked after a few moments' silence, looking up at the golden-haired older woman with the dangerous looking eyes. It was clear to see where Phoebe's good traits had come from but the girl's face was far smoother and more rounded than her mothers. A trait that definitely came from her father and gave her a much more refined look. Not that anyone couldn't say that Lucy Henderson wasn't refined but to Tony's eyes there was just something slightly special about the pale skinned, virtually white haired girl whom he had come to love.

"About you two moving in together down south…" Lucy's accent was thick with her Jamaican heritage. "Don't be so bloody silly. I know what young people get up to and I'm only thankful that I won't be worrying about some stupid little snobbish dancer trying to have his way with my little sugar ghost. I trust you, Tony. Just don't give me any details, okay? That's the last thing I need to hear about."

"Mum," Phoebe's voice cut in on the conversation, "are you trying to wind up Tony already?"

Standing in the doorway, framed by the rapidly fading sunlight which was burning a glorious yellow, red and pink across the sky, Phoebe looked like something out of a master class photography page. Tony wasted virtually no time in swivelling his camera around and pressing the rapid shutter button which would take lots of pictures of the same image but increase the sharpness, clarity and colours of each one. It was a gimmick that the camera boosted on its packaging but sometimes it proved to be one of the best things in the world. Phoebe was thankfully holding a bowl filled with a variety of chocolates and the dress strangely complimented her even paler-looking complexion. The ribbons in her hair had half-fallen out, leaving the coarse looking mess looking wild and untameable but with her hand on the door frame and a soft, rather surprised looking smile on her face the photo would look good. "Sometimes, I wish I had your abilities to create photos Phoebe, you're utterly brilliant," said Tony with a smile. "Though could you just step a little further into the doorway though? Just want to try and get some half descent shadows on your back."

Rolling her eyes with a sigh, Phoebe glanced to her mother who shrugged and chuckled before stepping just inside the doorway, automatically shifting her hand down so it was in a much more natural position. All three completely missed Alan's warning yell but when the shutter clicked, Amberly and Diesel somehow managed to line up perfectly around the girl's feet, carrying a pretend pumpkin barrel and a huge looking rubber bone in their mouths respectively. Bringing a hand covered in lace to her mouth, Phoebe chuckled at the pair and almost glared when the camera snapped once again but instead just turned it into a cheeky little look which clearly said, 'I'm going to get you for that one Tony George Richards'.

However before anything else could be said, or before anyone could have the chance to reply to Alan's ever increasing yell, an arm wound its way around Phoebe's middle causing her to tighten up just momentarily before the familiar tickle of warm breath ran across her neck and she felt the brush of slightly long hair. In the flash of the next photograph, taken completely by accident, the cat being from before appeared and bowed low to her for a mere instant and then faded just as fast as he came. Spinning around to push the figure away, Phoebe felt her heart stop beating for a few precious seconds.

The boy standing in front of her was tall, about a foot taller than her, finally out of his rather gangly looking phase with pale looking skin that matched hers and hair just a slightly darker shade of blond than it should have been. His brilliant blue eyes bore into hers, like looking into a mirror because they were so exact. For a moment she couldn't say a word but thankfully the young man just chuckled at her, running his fingers caringly down the side of her face. "Trick o' treat, twinny," John said briefly with a smile.

Chapter 4

Twin

It took around five very long seconds for Phoebe to be able to breathe again, let alone respond to the fact that she was once again looking at John. Almost instantly the memories came flooding back of the day she had last been able to spend with him but she was also aware of the other memories too. The ones that had happened but had never happened. How she had been there when he flew away to America to go and study abroad as he was so good at his astronomy and space age stuff that she couldn't even barely get her head around it. How he had tormented Alan to the point where the young boy had been sick, days in the park when he came home for holidays with the two dogs and all the rest of it. Throwing herself at the other, she buried her face into his jacket and smelt the all too familiar warmth that was her missing twin. "Hey, Rabbit," John said, hugging her back affection, "you're going to ruin the photo shoot if you start crying you silly thing."

Rallying fast, Phoebe pulled back and lightly punched her brother in the ribs. "You should have told me you were coming home then! I missed you so much you big jerk!" Tears were streaming down her face but John just wiped them away with his thumbs and shook his head at her. Though he didn't make any comments yet as he didn't want to, that would be saved for later on but it was surely such a great thing to see Phoebe again after so many years. He had been slightly worried when the child like angel had appeared to him once again but now he wasn't worried in the slightest. He too shared the memories that had flooded the girl's mind and wished that there were a way that he could keep them as precious gems to be viewed whenever he felt miserable or lonely.

"John," the other male in the room said, emphasising the word slowly to gain attention and also whine a question which he was sure that he knew the answer to, "when you're finished making my girlfriend cry can I borrow you for this photo?"

"No," John said immediately, turning his attention to Tony with a slight inclination of his eyebrow. "You know that I hate getting…"

"Oh, come on," Tony cut in once again. "This photo looks fantastic and I swear it'll do you the world of good."

"No! I've already said."

"Please?"

"How many times have I got to say it?"

"Will you do it for me?" Phoebe cut into the argument before it could escalate any further and make this whole session even longer than it needed to be. "Please, John, just this once?"

Her hand found his, locking their fingers together in a childish habit that she knew all too well he could barely refuse at the best of times. Her eyes bore into his, begging him to do this so that at least something might be salvaged at the end of the day. "I swear he won't put it up online – maybe in the shop or a magazine – but it's been such a long time since we had a photo together… plus I think Mum would like to look at one that was not that horrible school one."

"Speaking of mothers," – Lucy decided to make herself known to the group – "this one would like to actually get to hug her son if it can be so managed."

Slipping almost elegantly around Phoebe, John carefully avoided the dogs that were now fighting over the bone and hugged his mother with fondness and care. Taking her time to wipe away the tears which were still falling down her face, Phoebe got a good look at her bigger twin brother and saw why Tony said they would make a good picture. Whether he had intended to or not, John was dressed in a style which complimented her outfit almost perfectly. He wore a pair of simple black trousers with dark brown boots that were laced up with white laces, more than likely because John had broken the originals and not been able to find another set to match. His torso was covered with a much used, well-worn and battered looking dark brown flying jacket with soft cream inner lignin which Granda Micha had bought for him to go to the states with in order to deal with the 'Murky, freezing winters they get over there. Can't have my Grandson catching his death of cold out in Yankee Land – that just won't do' as Granda had said when he gave him the jacket.

No amount of convincing otherwise would tell the other that John wasn't going to the part of the states that really got affected by snow on a regular basis but it had been clearly set in stone in the old man's mind and once an idea was lodged there was no shifting it. Just visible underneath was a simple white shirt which

131

indicated that the boy had been travelling from some time and a golden chain which Phoebe had not seen before. Feeling Tony come up behind her and wrap his arms delicately around her frame, the dark haired boy leaned his chin on her shoulder and smiled. "Do you think he'll go for it?"

"Maybe," Phoebe said with a knowing smile. The twin lock was something that John could barely resist at the best of times. "But I'm not going to guarantee anything."

"I can hear you two, you know," John said before he sighed at the puppy dog look which the young girl was giving him. "Oh, all right, just this once because I owe you."

Giggling, Phoebe hugged her brother tightly and smiled. John glanced towards Tony. "Do I need anything else or will I be fine like this?"

Lucy cut in, virtually hauling John into a seat and immediately attacking his hair with the hairbrush she had been carrying before, "You'll let me attack that bonnet of yours, looks like it's been through a hedge backwards five times and don't think you're getting out of it young lady. I want you looking presentable for this photograph and Tony you had better give me the copies of the best one I'm telling you right now."

All three of the younger generation in the room exchanged a glance before rolling their eyes at one another. Half an hour later, both models were ready, John slightly hating the style his mother had forced upon him but putting up with it because he knew that he owed her a lot. Phoebe was thankfully much happier with hers as her hair had been simply put into two long glorious plates and decorated with the ribbons and a couple of silver cats which had been found after a good old fashioned rummage through the extra's box which Tony always brought with him.

Using the fireplace as a backdrop, Phoebe was seated in the chair with the pumpkin and the sweets resting perfectly on her knee. John was standing next to her, looking tall, proud and the typical lord of the manor, whilst Diesel sat firmly to attention next to him, the dog's black face and back adding a nice contrast to the white that stood out. Amberly, ever the one to pose for the camera, which had led to everyone believing that she was a reincarnation of some famous Hollywood actress of the nineteen fifties, managed to drape herself across the floor in front of Phoebe's feet looking like she was some prize winning show dog rather than a haphazard, hyperactive and mad Springer Spaniel who spent most of the day running around chasing after her brother and getting absolutely filthy.

Of course that was not the only photograph that was taken, they were shifted around in positioning, had to put up with the dogs rebelling at one point and deciding to have a play fight in the middle of everything but still somehow Tony got some really good pictures from them and of course the obligatory single shots of Phoebe to get the best angles on the dress she was wearing. Plus Alan decided that he wanted in on everything as well and came in dressed in his vampire Halloween costume which actually worked in context and after a little bit of persuading and convincing, they finally took a photograph of all of them together. It looked more like a promotional shot for a new series of *The Munsters* or something similar but it certainly looked fantastic.

"Heh, I'll have to bring the camera tomorrow night and try and get Scott and Penny in." Tony smiled as he went back through the pictures. "There's some really good ones on here."

"Don't forget Vincent," Lucy said with a smile. "We're picking him up from the airport tomorrow."

Tony scowled playfully. "Doesn't he get enough photos taken of himself already?"

John chuckled, as he took a long gulp of the pop he was drinking. "He would say the same thing Tony but he won't be happy unless he's in the photo as well. Trust me on that one."

Phoebe smiled happily, also taking a drink and glad that they had gotten in before the thunder and lightning had started. They were sitting in the kitchen and she so desperately wanted to talk to John about everything that had come before and what was going on now but knew it wasn't the right time. At least she would have all of her family around for Halloween, excluding her father which was a shame but there were just some things that couldn't happen in the slightest. Vaguely she wondered why she hadn't wished to see him but blinked as John ran his finger lightly over the back of her hand and smiled at her.

"Don't worry," he whispered, apparently able to read her thoughts from across the table, though that really didn't surprise her in the slightest since they were twins. "Things are going to be fun tomorrow."

Chapter 5

Reflections

The heat of the portable gas fire was pleasant and allowed Lucy some time to reflect on the quiet nature of the house. Tomorrow things were going to be stirred up to high chaos with not only Vincent but also Scott and Penny turning up, though thankfully they would be arriving in their own car. How both had managed to wrangle getting time off together was a mystery but considering the fact that they had a wedding to plan, there were probably a fair few strings pulled on both ends. Not that the blonde minded in the slightest. It would be nice to have a familiar, old fashioned noisy house back for a short time.

She always claimed to like the peace but in reality the ever busy woman despised it. In a lot of ways she was looking forward to starting her new job next year, it would take time away from the family granted but since Alan was getting to that age where he could look after himself it wouldn't be that much of a hassle. The book she was supposed to be reading lay idly in her hands, more resting than actually being read but that was the whole point of the thing. Every evening she came into the quiet living room and read for a while but tonight her thoughts wandered far and wide.

There was no particular form to them, just a gentle movement that swished and swirled about. Staring up at the ceiling, the mother side of her wondered about all of her children, who they would grow up to be and who they were going to marry. Vaguely she was aware that she appeared to know barely anything about John's school life but dismissed it incorrectly as being something to do with being highly over tired. She hadn't slept properly for the last few months, it felt strange to know that the other side of the bed was never going to be full again and strange, very surreal and frightening dreams had haunted her. But she wasn't going to dwell on those when there were many different things that she had to plan and be prepared for. Tomorrow was going to be a busy day, full of driving to the airport, cooking, cleaning, fixing costumes, bidding farewell to one life and beginning a new one.

"Lucy Henderson," she scolded herself in her best impression of Granda Micha, "stop fussing like an old mother hen. You're going to make yourself sick and that won't help you in the slightest."

Laughing loudly the woman gave up on her reading and instead went on her usual rounds of the bedrooms before retiring for the night. Alan was thankfully fast asleep, though as per usual his room looked like an utter bombsite but that was just the way that the eight-year-old lived at the moment. Though upon closer inspection, the utter mess actually transpired to be some form of elaborate game with robotic fighters facing off against one another. There were plenty of causalities clearly and some would only come back from the brink when the child decided that he wanted to play a different game but the ever keen eyed mother realised that the toys which had been bought by Vincent were settled on the highest shelf not to be played with. A smile crossed her face as Lucy gentle tiptoed through the room to tuck her son in for the night and place a kiss on his forehead.

"Alan, you're such a terror but I love you," she whispered, receiving a half groan in response which was good enough for her.

Getting out of the room, Lucy sighed at the pleading look in both dog's eyes but firmly shook her head at them, "You can stay with one of the twins but not Alan, I'm not having him anymore hyperactive than he needs to be tomorrow and it's no use pulling the puppy dog expression either."

The two dogs just continued to look at her with an expression of total misunderstanding but Lucy just rolled her eyes skyward and headed towards the other bedrooms. They were just up the stairs, but sometimes Lucy really wished she had held out against her now departed husband in the purchase of the place. It was an old Victorian style house with four storeys all together, including the ground floor, and had its fair share of problems for being such an old building. Thankfully the repairs were easy to recover with grants and the fact that they still had plenty of money to spare but sometimes the matriarchal mother felt that things were just a little bit too big for the family.

The ground floor held a large open plan kitchen diner which had plenty of original features that worked perfectly well and were never changed. Well excluding the introduction of a washing machine and dryer because Lucy refused to use the two tub system and ringer. They had gone to an antiques dealer years ago and fetched a nice little price for a museum. There were also two living rooms, a fairly roomy cupboard which housed most of the knick-knacks that couldn't be placed anywhere else and an old grandfather clock which ticked away into the night.

The first floor held Alan's room, the first bathroom, a study and a room which had originally been a library but had been converted into a sort of general family room that one hour could be a child's playroom but the next be a quiet reading space, a dance practice hall or any number of things. It didn't have a proper title; it was just the room where you went if everywhere else in the house was taken up. The second floor held pretty much the same allocation of rooms but these were given over to the older children. Vincent still had his own room though it frequently doubled as a guest room and was generally left rather bare and tidy. The twins each had a room, the doors exactly opposite one another and laid out in a virtual mirror image. Of course as they had grown up, their tastes had changed dramatically but the furniture was always laid out the same, no matter which way it was moved.

Scott also had a room up on this floor, it was at the end opposite the bathroom and it was the largest which served its purpose well because the young man had seriously gotten into his weight training when he was around twelve years old and had a small portion sectioned off where an exercise bike, several weights and a strange toning machine were standing waiting to be taken away to the couples new home. How Penny was going to put up with her boyfriend's constant work out was a mystery to Lucy but then she did remember the fact that girls liked their guys to work out. Oh, it was completely hopeless – trying to think like a teenager these days but that wasn't going to disturb the mother's thoughts right now. There was a big bathroom on this floor as well, with a modern day suite in it and plenty of room to accommodate four rowdy teenagers who all needed to use the space.

The topmost floor of the house had at one time been an attic where odds and ends were stored but as the family number increased, it had eventually become the master bedroom, bathroom and reclusive living room/study that were completely kid free. Even to this day, Scott wasn't permitted in the room despite the fact that he had long ago passed the necessary age and maturity levels to be considered a 'kid'. Rules were rules in this house and that was how it was going to remain. Sometimes Lucy did wonder why she clung to such old fashioned ideals but sometimes it was still nice to just have a place to retreat to. She knew for certain that she would need it when her mother-in-law inevitably turned up sometime tomorrow but at least the old bint would have the semi-decency to get a taxi here.

Pulling out of her wanderings, Lucy knocked gently on the door which led to Phoebe's room and popped her head around the corner. "Hi, honey, just doing my rounds before I retire for the night. Everything okay in here?"

"Yes, Mum, it is," Phoebe replied, looking at her mother from under the hem of a green towel which she was using in order to dry her hair, "and before you ask, no he's not hidden under the bed or in the closet or anything like that."

Lucy managed to pull off a horrified looking face despite the fact that she was trying not to laugh at her daughter's remarks, the girl clearly knew her all too well. "I wasn't even going to suggest such a thing. I know that Tony's a very respectable young gentleman and wouldn't think of anything so crass or so crude."

Giving her mother a look which plainly said 'yeah right' but not actually voicing the thought aloud, the girl was glad that she could go back to drying her hair to avoid that topic of conversation. She had unfortunately had to listen to Scott going through the same talk and quite frankly the very idea of doing so again was enough to make her run to the hills. Lucy's version of the birds and the bees made the school's rather graphic picture books look like a walk in the park in comparison. It wasn't that the woman wanted to scare her children but Lucy had definitely walked on the wild side of life and knew a fair few things about it. Getting the hint, Lucy chuckled at her daughter, "Okay, I understand when I'm not wanted. Don't stay up too late, sweetheart. We've got an early start in the morning and I'm sure that Vincent doesn't want to be greeted by someone who's half asleep."

Phoebe snorted at her mother. "He'll be the one who's half asleep, Mum. He'll have barely been off the stage more than an hour before he gets on that flight and won't have slept like any sane person would do because of that stupid fear of his."

Vincent didn't have a fear of flying; he just had a fear that someone was going to hijack the plane and threaten to kill them all if he fell asleep. It was due to some strange movie he had watched years ago and it had never really registered in the young man's head that it was all fake. There again, Vincent had believed – or at least claimed to – in Santa Clause until he was thirteen and a half. She did love her brother but sometimes his idiocy seemed so misplaced that she had to wonder about him.

"Oh leave him be," Lucy said. "You're over the moon that he's back and don't you deny it, missy. Anyway, I'm going to check on John now and then go to bed. Pleasant dreams."

"Night, Mum," Phoebe called, waiting until the door was closed before dropping the dry towel into the basket and wandering over to the night stand in order to brush her blonde hair. She would wait a good half hour before creeping to her twin's bedroom to talk as she knew automatically that neither of them would be sleeping very well tonight.

Lucy found John in his usual position by the window, looking through one of his many telescopes and recording data on some planet or constellation or something similar. For a moment it felt extremely strange being in the room and her eyes wandered around it curiously. The furniture was nearly identical to Phoebe's but decked out mainly in a darker colour with dark blue bed sheets and a lighter blue on the walls. The floor was a murky grey colour but it was the ceiling that most enchanted her. It was a dark black and had the star charts of the milky-way painted on it. She remembered how it had taken forever and a day to do but somehow even after several years of artificial lights and different furniture it still managed to look absolutely stunningly wonderful.

"You all right, Mum?" John asked, having noticed that his mother was in the room long before she had even really registered where he was. Blinking, Lucy found herself having to crane her neck ever so slightly in order to see her son better than before and smiled lightly up at him. Finally he had stopped appearing tall and lanky, with gangly limbs that didn't match his posture very well. John looked like a blond version of his dad, just with smoother features and far more smiley lines as the woman liked to call them. For a moment, her mothering instincts thought back to the unsure days in the hospital, just after the operation which might kill both of her babies and looking in on the special cribs with that knowing feeling that only one would live.

It had been horrible and nearly reduced her to tears every time she thought about it but looking at her son, she wondered for a moment why she had been convinced that she would lose one of them. Lightly she shook her head. "Yes, everything's all right, John. I guess I'm just getting stressed about tomorrow."

Smiling, the boy took her into his arms and held her tightly. Far more tightly than he ever would have done in the past but Lucy wasn't bothered by such actions. She held him back, glad to hold him once again before laughing. "Oh if your Granda could see me now, he would call me a wet wimp and send me off to bed." Tears were inexplicably rolling down her face and quickly she removed them with the corner of her sleeve, "In fact I'm going to send myself off to bed before I end up blubbering like some fish out of the sea. Don't stay up to late… oh wait you already know that bit."

Placing a kiss on his cheek, Lucy quickly hurried off to go and take a long hot shower before going to sleep. She had no idea what was wrong with her but all she knew was that it was better to clear her head and work out things on her own. Though for once she really wished that she didn't have to do so.

John, still standing in his bedroom, looked down at his hands before bringing them close to his chest as he closed his eyes. He was fighting against the waves of pain that were reverberating through his body and he couldn't understand why this situation hurt so much as it did. Sitting down on the bed, he sighed and shook his head, remembering what Terry had said to him the other day. "Of course it's going to hurt, it'll never stop hurting but if you remember only the good times then the pain will lessen eventually."

For a second he wondered if the other would be in this place and figured that it was more than likely. He would have to send an e-mail or a text tomorrow and introduce this family to Terry. It would certainly be an experience indeed. Though as he glanced to the clock on his bedside table, the young man figured that he only had a window of about twenty minutes before Phoebe would come sneaking across and it was a conversation that he was both looking forward to and dreading at the same time.

Walking to his wardrobe, John quickly ran his hands through the pile of clothes on the top shelf until he felt the familiar warmth of the wooden box with the dragons on it. For once he didn't take the object out, just left it where it was because he knew that he couldn't read the book Phoebe had written in right now. For a moment he wondered if she had ever read his but decided not to ask. Plus he had stars to monitor at the moment, so he sat back down at his telescope and slowly began the methodical record keeping which was part homework, part hobby.

Chapter 6

Star Light, Star Bright

Not looking up from his complicated record chart when the door opened, John focused for a few more tentative seconds on the small sector of space that he was currently gazing at before quietly finishing his recording. He wasn't being rude at all, it was just that his observations had to go undisturbed to be regarded as accurate and technically he had cheated on the time scales purely so that he could get away with having Halloween off. Not that his tutors would think anything of it, as far as they were concerned John was already far above most of the other students, if not all given two exceptions in the entire year group, and definitely had more than enough star data recorded to fill at least three books worth of information.

If truth be told however, John had a lot more star chart information than that. Throughout the whole of the house were a massive collection of books, note pads and art pads which were just filled with records of the stars and accurate maps that charted the course of asteroids, meteor showers and the occasional comet. He had been serious about taking up astronomy full time when he was eight years old and the hobby had slowly become an obsession which then began to over flow into all the possibilities of a potential career in one of the greatest projects on Earth. But that was by the by right now, he had to focus on what was on this very small, blue green planet considered to be somewhere in the vicinity of the star system of Betelgeuse. Leastways that was the case if you happened to read rather humorous science fiction books in-between some serious studying.

Phoebe regarded him with confused eyes, seemingly caught between two distinct emotions at the same time. John could easily sympathise with her plight as he fully understood what she was going through. Lightly he sighed, "I read your book, you know. The old battered leather thing… I read it every night trying to discern just who you were. Are you sure you don't want to go into journalism rather than dancing, Phoebe? You would suit the style very well."

The girl shook her head lightly, her blonde hair flowing across her shoulders like a river. "No, I chose dance a long time ago and I'm going to see it through to the very end. I know it's something that I can't do forever but it's my passion in life and even if I just get to be a choreographer in the end I shall be happy."

They lapsed into silence once again, each one thinking the same worrisome thoughts but not quite prepared to voice the words aloud. "I missed…" Both broke into quiet laughter at realising that they were speaking at the same time and their eyes met. Suddenly everything seemed to fall into place and it was John who crossed the gap between them first to pull the girl into a hug and spin her around. "I wish that I could never forget you,

Phoebe." He smiled, running his hands through her hair. "You mean the world to me."

"Wishes like ours are only temporary, you know that," the female twin replied, running her hand instinctively down her brother's left hand side to feel the scars along them. "I never even dreamed that we would get another chance like this."

"Maybe there's a reason for it," John said with a smile, still holding her close, "but at least we can enjoy this time together once again."

Phoebe gave him a sharp look, "Have you ever been around our house at Halloween?"

The general consensus of Halloween in the Henderson household was that virtually everyone, with the current exception of Alan and the two dogs, was glad when the whole thing was done and dusted. It wasn't the fact that they didn't like spending time together as one big, noisy and very happy family, it was the fact that guaranteed Grandmother Christine would turn up and sour everything down, spoil Alan with sweets that sent him up the wall to hyper point, kick the dogs and generally spoil everything else. It was the one 'holiday' that they had to put up with the old bat, as she was often referred to around the house, because her other daughter – Aunt Margareta – who was the absolute apple of her mother's eyes, as well as the one who was virtually a spitting image of her, did not believe in celebrating the holiday.

Margareta was extremely condescending of anything that did not have church approval and refused at all levels to have anything to do with her brother's family. The whole affair was actually over the fact that Lucy and Jeff had decided, of their own free will, to marry in Jamaica in a traditional themed wedding conducted by the priest who had married Granda Micha and Grandma Hannah and baptized Lucy when she was a baby. The whole day had been one big celebration, inside and outside of the little church but Margareta was convinced that it was not the proper thing to do and had virtually disowned them since. In a lot of ways everyone was thankful for the fact but it unfortunately meant that they had to put up with Grandmother Christine causing utter hell for them all.

"Of course I have," sighed John with a grin, "but I can't think of anywhere else I would rather be. Plus you get to escape to that ball with a certain someone."

"Oh shut up." Phoebe was blushing nearly crimson which did not look healthy in the slightest and she tried to pull herself out of her twin's embrace. "I'm going to have more than enough troubles with Scott and Vincent going on at me tomorrow without you adding to the mix!"

Chuckling, John pulled the girl back in closer to his body. "Oh, come on, I've got more than enough right to ask all about this guy. I've got some vague memories of him at the moment but I don't know him in the slightest... and plus I did promise to look after you."

Phoebe rolled her eyes and tried to pull away from him again but all it ended up in was a friendly tussle back and forth before she managed to skilfully hook her leg around his knee and kick out. It was a simple dance move which she had learnt a long time ago could be very useful for getting out of these sorts of situations but unfortunately for the girl, the boy kept hold as they crashed onto the bed which thankfully didn't make any form of noise on the room below. Giggling, Phoebe continued to struggle out of the other's grip but had to concede in the end because it was just easier to do. "Gah! You're worse than Vincent and that's saying something, John!" she playfully growled at the other, though couldn't hide the smile on her face.

"Oh, come on," John whined, loosening his hold but placing his hands so that he could tickle the girl if she resisted him any further. Instinctively he knew that she was susceptive to tickling and it was a safe ploy to use. "I promise I won't rip the guy to pieces or anything. He seems really nice, actually."

For a moment she considered backing out but decided against it, there was a look in the other's eyes which told her that he knew a fair trick or two which could make her talk and the last thing she needed right now was for their mother to come downstairs to enquire what was going on. It would of course be perfectly normal to find the twins sharing a bed, they had done before on so many occasions but it was still a rather delicate subject. Lucy knew that there was nothing going on between them but she preferred to err on the side of caution. Letting out a theatrical sigh of defeat she glared at her twin, "All right, I'll tell you what you want to know but you've got to trade with me to make it fair."

John, not thinking things through at this precise moment in time, nodded gleefully and snuggled closer to his sister. "No problems, what trade subject?"

"You tell me about your gi—" cutting herself off, the blonde-haired girl thought things through before suddenly letting out a knowing chuckle. "Your boyfriend."

"How the hell did?" John started before catching himself and groaning. Of course Phoebe would know about Terry, he would have told her because he would want her opinion first on the whole situation. He hadn't told anyone else in the family, partially due to the fact that he wasn't sure how they were going to react and also because he was still a little insecure with the thought himself. The man wasn't his first love or anything like that, John was a bit more experienced than he would ever willingly admit to his mother or father, but it was still just something that he couldn't quite work out.

It was all down to a biology class which had talked about attraction from a molecular level, how males and females were naturally attracted to one another but if a certain imbalance was present then it was also perfectly natural for males and females to be attracted to the same sex. John had rather taken the session to heart, wondering if the reason he liked boys was due to the fact that he was born a girl originally or not and despite the fact that he had dated two others before Terry, he was still a little unsure of himself. Granted, his boyfriend knew of the worry and tried to help him through it as much as he possibly could but sometimes it was a bit of a barrier between them.

Phoebe ran her hand through the other's blond hair and sighed. "You are such a worry pot, John. You know that? It doesn't matter about what gender you like; it just matters that you love them very much."

"You know, this whole mind-reading thing is really annoying," the boy replied, idly running his fingers down Phoebe's side though not enough to elicit a response from her as of yet.

Nodding, the girl chuckled. "Of course I know, right now we've spent our lives together so we pretty much know each other inside out."

"That's a horrible mental image I didn't need." The cheeky reply was met with a sharp thwack to the head which only increased the laughter somewhat. John sighed. "Okay, okay... I guess I'm just worried how everyone will take to the fact I'm gay is all."

For a few seconds there was silence, followed by a sigh. "That's one hell of a way to get out of talking about him," Phoebe said knowingly before staring up at the ceiling, "but to be truthful, I think Mum will be really cool with it. Scott probably won't be surprised in the slightest considering he's virtually watched you growing up and knows more stories than even I could put together. Vincent will be chuffed to mint-balls and will probably try to use the pair of you in one of his random video blogs or something along those lines." Vincent lived with a gay guy in Japan and loved having him around because he was the best stylist which made looking gorgeous even easier for him. "Alan won't have a flipping clue as per usual, the dogs will just look at you blankly and then try to get you to play with them, Granda Micha will be supportive as he always is and Grandmother..."

"Will be Grandmother about the whole thing?" John finished, sighing and shaking his head. "I was hoping to not have to face her any time soon."

"We all were," Phoebe said with a roll of her eyes. "Now, you tell me all about Terry and I'll tell you all about Tony."

John smiled faintly for a moment before suddenly frowning. "We've really got to stop this twin thing. I'm dating a guy with a name beginning with T and you're also dating a guy with a name beginning with T. It's going to get really confusing."

Phoebe grinned. "Well as long as yours doesn't have black hair, isn't a Goth with plans to open a Gothic Lolita store in London and takes photographs of pretty girls wearing his creations I think we'll be okay."

There was a pause before John chuckled. "Thankfully we're chalk and cheese there. Terry's a seven foot tall brunette who plays for the school basketball team, has no idea that Scotland is connected to England and wants nothing more than to open his own day-care centre once he graduates from his business degree."

"Wow," Phoebe said, "talk about picking the odd one of the lot, John."

For a few moments the pair slipped into silence, just listening to the general emptiness of the house around them and musing on life. "Hey, Phoebe," John said at length.

"Yeah?"

"Where's Dad?"

"He was in a coma the last time you came to my world," came the sad reply. "He couldn't support himself anymore so Mum had to make the choice. He passed on around seven months ago now."

"Would you like to see him again?" The whisper was low and a little bit unsure, almost as if things weren't happening that were supposed to be.

Phoebe was quiet once again, thinking things through and staring at the star chart above her. "I suppose so," she said at length before smiling. "Actually, yes I would like to see him once again."

John smiled secretly to himself. "Good. Now, about Tony?"

The rest of the night fizzled away into a quiet stream of conversation which only ended when both were unable to keep their eyes open any longer.

Chapter 7

Airports

If there was possibly anything more boring in existence than sitting waiting for a delayed plane then none of the Henderson's knew what it could possibly be. Things had been relatively fine at first, everyone had woken up at a reasonable time and was ready to go with five minutes to spare which was virtually unheard of. They had even managed to get through the often crazy rush hour traffic reasonably well which was something that just never happened for them. It was slightly disconcerting to arrive well before the middle brother and not have him moan on cue that he had been standing around for hours when in fact it had only been a few moments. Still at least they had managed to grab some chairs whilst they waited in the arrivals area, which was better than having to constantly stand all the time.

Lucy had wandered off after ten minutes, purely to check that the plane was due in on time as that was the one thing she forgot to do and had discovered that the flight had been forced to land in Switzerland due to a freak bout of weather. So duly, Vincent was running two hours late which proved to be more of a hassle than anything else to the family. Thankfully with the twins around, Alan was easy enough to control and entertain so Lucy got the rare opportunity to sit and have a cup of tea in peace and quiet whilst she tried once again to get her son on the phone to check that everything was all right. It was rare that the young man didn't have his phone switched on, ready to answer in case something came up but either he was out of signal or had been given some form of sedative in order to make him sleep. Lucy had a feeling that it would be the second option as after having managed to have a slightly broken conversation with his manager, she had learned that his fear of being hijacked was now turning into just a general fear of flying which was not going to be an easy situation to deal with.

Still at least the children were out of her hair and in reach by phone, so as soon as she knew that the plane was in then the three that were with her could just come straight back. In order to keep the young child happy, the small group had wandered off to a very noisy arcade where there were lots of bright machines with their strange games, some very simple children's things and a few other odds and ends. It wouldn't keep Alan entertained for long but it was a starting point at the very least. Thankfully they had some spare change between them so playing the games wasn't going to be that big a problem, just choosing something was proving that way and the age appropriate games were less appealing than the other types. Their first stop, typically as always, was the DDR machine where they all had at least one go at trying to beat the top score.

Amazingly it was only Alan who got anywhere near close as both of the twins were more interested in just enjoying the music rather than actually paying attention to what they were doing. That was until a random selection of the song 'Butterfly' came up again and then the match was on. "Equal points again!" Phoebe said in complete disbelief. "That song is officially jinxed against us."

"Well considering how often we've actually played that one it's not that surprising. We should try it on hard mode," John said, though he was panting heavily by now and was rather glad that there weren't more people to see them making a fool of themselves.

"No!" Alan moaned. "I want to play on something else. This is boring." The eight-year-old's excuse wasn't actually meant of course, Alan did love these sort of games but there were much more exciting games to play in this arcade than just DDR. There was a minor disagreement between the siblings about what should be played next, as the younger had spotted a shooting game called *House of the Dead* and wanted a go but neither of his elder brother or sister wanted to give him the mildest shot had having nightmares. Thankfully they had found a dinosaur river race game which required a bit of team work to get going properly and turned out to be a really good ride. Granted, they got eaten more times than they could possibly count but it certainly entertained.

Moving on, Phoebe helped Alan to win some more coins for the machine through the lucky drop penny machine. The girl had always had outstanding luck with those machines and they quickly gathered up the change which was a hefty sum and turned it into more pound coins. John in the meantime had a go on Time Splitters another shooting game but this one was more easily within the safe realm of age ranges. When Alan realised he demanded to have go and therefore a good ten minutes passed playing the game. There wasn't much else to do after that, so they decided to wander around the closest shop that was built into the airport to see if they could find any magazines or newspapers to read.

"I'll just be a moment," John called to the disappearing figures of Phoebe and Alan, as he ducked into an alcove which was not that visible after being in the darkened arcade with all its bright lights. His attention had been caught by a claw game and since it was six goes for one pound, how that worked out he didn't quite know, but he wasn't about to argue. John always loved claw games, ever since he was a child, and always gave them a go. Yes, he knew they were rigged and extremely tricky and were generally a waste of money but he just adored them. This one contained a selection of glittering watches and jewellery, clearly all fake but nice looking at the same time. There were a couple of toy based ones but he had dismissed them purely on instinct.

Putting the money into the machine, the young man began his careful game of trying to grab the items and found that some high deity had blessed his game. Every single go he managed to win something which brought a smile to his face and he carefully collected them at the end with reverence. Automatically he decided not to tell the others quite yet of his luck and placed the items securely in his inner coat pocket before hearing his mobile ringing. Digging it out of his pocket, John smiled to himself when he saw the caller ID saying 'Mum' and answered, "I take it the plane's in?"

"Yes, it's just landed so you'll have more than enough time to get back here." Lucy's voice came back over the other end of the phone. "Don't take too long though, I think he might be in a state."

"No problem, I'll just fetch Alan and Phoebe and we'll be back shortly. See you soon." John spoke with a happy sigh before hanging up and heading to the shop. It wasn't a big place, just more of a glorified magazine stand but that didn't matter overly much. Phoebe was just paying for the purchases whilst Alan was trying to sneak off but John spotted him and quickly picked the lad up. "Ha! Got you."

"Aww! Put me down!" Alan moaned, trying to wriggle his way out but only found himself safely turned upside down which caused the blond-haired boy to squeal but thankfully not loudly which was a good thing.

Phoebe smiled at her brother. "Thanks, I was beginning to think that I wouldn't be able to catch him if he ran off. Mum called I take it?"

John nodded, righting Alan but keeping a hold of him. "Yup. Don't we have some reigns or something for this one? It would make life a whole lot easier."

Returning to their mother, the family only had to wait about fifteen minutes extra for Vincent to come through the arrivals doorway. To be brutally truthful the just-turned seventeen-year-old looked an absolute wreck. There were big dark circles under his eyes, he was dressed in an oversized T-shirt with the biggest coat he could find wrapped around him and appeared to be still in the somewhat process of trying to wake up and be coherent enough. Of course he greeted his family with his usual dazzling smile and happy go lucky attitude but it wasn't long before the boy was nearly tripping over his feet.

"You know for once I'm really glad you are taller than me," Vincent said with a heavy yawn as he rested against John who simply rolled his eyes at Phoebe. The girl was happy to have her younger brother back but was slightly worried about his condition. Normally sleeping pills didn't have this sort of reaction on Vincent, in fact he had to be taken off them and given a very strict and disciplined routine on tour last year because he was starting to become heavily addicted to them but as she hugged him for a second time, she felt heat coming from his body despite the fact that he was shaking like a leaf.

"Vinny," she scolded automatically, realising the reason for her brother coming home, "you stupid nitwit! You shouldn't have travelled when you're this bad."

Vincent half glowered at his sister but shook his head. "I was fine when we left Tokyo, it was when we got to thingy that I started to feel like this."

John sighed, "Well you best not give it to any of us, that's the last thing we need with everything else at the moment. Where's Mum?"

"Talking to Tamara-san," replied Alan, coming back with a juice drink for Vincent who took it happily. "She'll be back in a minute."

Lucy was back not thirty seconds later and they quickly bundled the teenager into the back of the car and loaded his bags into the boot. With the extra body in the back seat it was a bit more of a cosy set up but no one minded. They were barely out of the airport before Vincent was slumbering against John's shoulder whilst holding onto Alan. Feeling a little bit mischievous, Phoebe dug out her new camera and managed to get a sneaky photo of the group which resulted in her receiving the 'V' sign from her slightly sick brother followed by a round of laughter.

Chapter 8

Chip Sandwiches

The drive back towards home was thankfully not too long but the family took the usual detour via the local chip shop to get Vincent his most favourite food. For a grand total of one pound and fifty pence, they purchased a very large chip butty. Quite as to why Vincent liked such things was a subject open to debate but it was part of the tradition of the boy being back in his home town. That and of course getting the opportunity to live life relatively normally for a few short hours or weeks as this visit was transpiring to be. Sometimes the other would complain about the celebrity life that he had to live in Japan because he had so much to do but it was more of a token argument.

"At least you're looking a bit perkier now," Phoebe said, swinging her legs back and forth whilst she waited with Vincent outside for the order to be brought out to them. "I was beginning to worry that you would be sick in the car there."

Vincent chuckled. "It's only tour buses that I'm sick on now... it's not a pleasant thing in the slightest."

Shaking her head so her blonde hair swished back and forth, Phoebe couldn't help but feel a mixture of pity, sorrow and disbelief for her younger brother. He had the life which most boys could only aspire to and yet there were always things that plagued him about it. He had an aversion to travel which caused him to be very unwell on a lot of occasions, there were more times than she could count when he had suffered from a horrible bout of homesickness which frequently resulted in her being on the phone to him at three o'clock in the morning when she had an important dance recital or exam looming and recently he had developed a quirk which meant that he would momentarily forget how to speak Japanese. She was positive that there was something highly wrong with the other, as there was no way that he should be acting like this but getting alone time with the other was a hard thing to do.

"Vincent," she started, pausing only briefly to work out how to phrase things in her head, "what on earth is wrong with you? Over the past six months you've become a right depressing lout and even the fan girls over here are commenting on it. You're not eating – that much I can tell just by looking at you – you're grouchy and you've come down with a cold. You never come down with a cold unless it's something highly contagious like chicken pox." Phoebe remembered that incident a little too well as she had ended up looking like a target practice map during the whole time and had to engage in a stupid game of join-the-dots with the camomile lotion in order to get Alan to be willing to put the stuff on. "And don't try to back out of it either, young man. I'm your big sister and I worry about you."

Raising his eyes to his sister's blue ones, Vincent smiled sadly at her before looking down at the ground once again. "I don't know where to even begin. It's stupid… even you'll laugh when you hear about it."

"Try me," Phoebe said, wishing that the problem wasn't something along the lines that he had gotten some girl pregnant. That would be a big problem that couldn't be resolved by just talking about it. Something told her that it wasn't anything like that, thankfully, but she was careful about believing in such instincts right now.

"Not here," Vincent replied, resting his head on her shoulder whilst she wrapped her arms around him. "I don't want them to hear and start fussing."

Glancing into the shop, which was absolutely heaving due to two of the cookers being off, the girl shook her head again. "Don't worry about them, Vinny, they'll be in there ages yet. Looks like they haven't fixed the cookers so they are having to do things in the small one which takes forever and a day regardless. Come on, tell me what's bothering my little brother."

Feeling the white fingers running through his dark, unruly hair, Vincent considered the options for a few long moments. To have someone to confide in would be a wonderful thing but he had no idea about how his sister would respond. It wasn't the sort of problem that could just be worked out overnight and he knew that he was being a total fool over the whole situation but as far as he was concerned there was no magical path to follow. Finally he decided it would be best to just get it out of the way and quietly he wrapped his arms around Phoebe before letting out a sigh. "It's Kirei," he started, wincing slightly at even saying the name. "I just don't know what to do!"

Phoebe had to think for a few seconds about who Kirei was – she was often hopeless with remembering all of Vincent's Japanese friends but a sudden image flashed through her mind of a motorbike and a glamorous smile. "The Racer?" she asked, just to clarify with the other who nodded in response. "What's wrong with him?"

Vincent fell quiet, not quite ready to speak but knowing he had to. "Nothing… well, not quite. He fell off his bike a few months ago during a race and it was a horrible crash and they think he's going to be in hospital a long time and it's touch and go if he will be able to walk again let alone ride and it's his life." Phoebe let her brother twitter on, knowing fine well that this was not the main reason for her brother's distress. It was definitely part of it but it only added to the bigger picture. "I think I caused the crash."

"You?" Caught genuinely by surprise, Phoebe looked down at Vincent with a frown. "How could you be the cause of the crash? You were nowhere near that part of the race track at the time." It was John and Scott who were into their motorbike racing and it wasn't uncommon to find the pair watching the live races at stupid o'clock in the morning in the living room, hence why she recognised the situation and remembered seeing the crash which had been horrific at the time. "They said it was due to excess oil on the track." Though a sudden dread started in her stomach as the boy increased his grip on it ever so slightly.

"I know." Vincent was virtually whining at this point in time. "But just before the race… Kirei… said… admitted s-some…"

Smiling gently, Phoebe knew her fears were confirmed. "He told you the truth, didn't he?"

There was no verbal response, just a tightening of the hold and the girl sighed before resting her chin on his head. She knew what should be said right now but didn't want to cause anymore tears to fall from the boy's eyes below as they were already soaking her top.

"You panicked, right?" came another voice and both jumped up in surprise to find Scott smiling down at them with a knowing look on his features. "Probably said something stupid like you weren't looking for a relationship or weren't gay?"

"How did?" started Vincent, who was cut off by Phoebe's question of, "Where did you appear from?"

Shaking his head at the pair, Scott pulled them both into a tight embrace. "Is that what I get after all these months? No 'Oh, Scott, it's wonderful to see you, how are you, big brother?' What do I get? Where did you appear from and how did I know what my younger twerp of a brother was going to respond with?"

"Stop teasing," Phoebe said pulling back to get a good look at her older brother who still managed to look fantastic which annoyed the heck out of her. All of her brothers, excluding Alan who was just at that stage of being cute, were fit looking men with dazzling smiles and had girls – or boys – throwing themselves at them. She always felt the odd one out, rather plain by comparison but if anyone had ever asked one of her brothers they would have said that their sister was the prettiest out of all of them. Sibling rules were always a complicated situation to deal with but it was how life was no matter what the circumstances.

Scott grinned. "Well to respond to your question, sis, quite simply I came from home with Penny when I realised that you lot were still picking up this little squirt here and I know you only too well Vincent. You didn't cause that crash and the fact that you are in the process of making yourself absolutely sick over his

163

health and this situation clearly says that you care deeply for this fellow."

Shaking his head in response, Vincent sighed. "But I've been so mean to him. There's no way I can just go back and... you know?"

"Confirm what every fan girl thinks and stop those pretty horrible fan fictions that have you and Karamu together all the time?" John's voice cut in, along with the smell of fresh chip butties which were smothered in butter and steaming hot. "Mam spotted your car from the window Scott and has an order on the go. Means we'll have a few extra minutes here."

Vincent took his sandwich before looking up at John, "Why are you reading those sorts of fictions, John?"

Rolling his eyes skyward whilst trying to hide the fact that he was choking on a particularly hot chip, Scott sighed. "John's been into... what the hell is it called? Oh yoyo, yaow." Faltering desperately, the other waved his hand about in a manner which clearly said he was confused.

"Yaoi," Phoebe replied with a knowing grin and a shrug towards John.

Scott clicked his fingers. "Thank you, Phoebe, since he was about ten years old. I spotted that you shared similar traits with him when you were about seven years old, Vinny. It's no big surprise to me, same with John."

Butty half way to his mouth, John glared at his older brother. "You've been reading my diary again, haven't you?"

"Nope," Scott replied, tapping the side of his head. "It doesn't take a lot to work out if you open your eyes and use your noggin."

164

Looking down at his sandwich, Vincent smiled before looking up at John still a little shy and nervous, "I don't know if I can come out... it's going to cause utter hell no matter what."

"Well, take it like this: we'll both come out together, okay?" John smiled, digging Phoebe in the ribs to stop her saying anything. "Plus, I'm sure your fans will love the photo opportunities and I bet Kirei will be happier for it."

Nodding quietly, Vincent smiled and took a bite out of the sandwich whilst he was caught into a big three way hug by his older siblings. It was going to be a tricky situation and he was sure that there was going to be questions but the sixteen-year-old knew that if he didn't do it soon then it would be exposed in a really shattering way which could wreck his career. He felt thankful for having such understanding siblings and was even more pleased that he wasn't the only one in the family who batted for the other team. Now that he thought about it, he should have really realised a whole lot earlier but he had been so caught up in his own worries that he had not paid proper attention.

"I hope you still want me, Kirei," he whispered to himself, enveloped in the big hug, "because I want you more than ever right now. I'll talk to you soon. I swear it."

Chapter 9

Grandmother

The rest of the journey back was conducted with as little hassle as possible, simply because everyone was happily munching on their sandwiches and trying to just enjoy the time that they had together. Vincent was still a little bit on the unsure side of course but since he had the support of all of his older siblings he was smiling a lot more and it was easy to see that a great weight had been lifted from his shoulder's which was a good thing. The car drove along perfectly fine, thankfully the traffic wasn't busy in the slightest and things just appeared to go from good to better. Lucy put the radio on and the songs played got the whole family singing completely out of tune and as loudly as possible which caused a fair few interesting looks to come their way from passers-by but most just shook their heads and kept on going.

As they were half way through the song 'Living on a Prayer', the two cars pulled into their street and almost instantly the smile fell from Lucy's face. There was a black car parked outside of their house, a taxi thankfully but one which sent shivers down her spine. There was only one woman in the world who would ordain to come and visit them in a black hackney cab and that was Grandmother Christina. Already she could feel the waves of unspoken hatred coming from the back seat because they had ordained to make her wait and pay extra for the taxi service. "Oh here we go," she said aloud without meaning, which made everyone focus on the cab.

Automatically there were a variety of suppressed groans and moans from the others but they knew how to act in this situation. It was something that they had all learned to cope with a long time ago; even the youngest Alan was on good behaviour when the severe looking older woman was around. Normally they wouldn't be graced with her presence until at least six o'clock, so it was presumable that she was having an argument with someone on her street and did not wish to see them for the whole day. Vincent groaned and lowered his head. "Can't I just claim to be sick and hide in my room for the rest of the day?"

"Don't be so selfish," his mother replied. "I wish we all could do that but it's not going to happen. Come on, let's go and face the music."

As she climbed out of the car, Phoebe noticed that John had been rather quiet throughout the whole situation, only letting out a token groan every now and then. It was odd because she knew that John was generally the one to hold the peace during these situations because he was one of the only family members who had truly faced her wrath head on and managed to live. Granted it wasn't in the easiest of circumstances but he was still here and knew a thing or two. No one could remember what the argument had been about, nor why it had really occurred, but John had certainly put in his penny's worth and got a whole lot out of it.

Unfortunately ever since, Grandmother Christina had been doubly cruel to the lad, not that she was especially nice to anyone else unless there was a specific reason behind it of course. It was then that she noticed that he was texting on his mobile phone and had a small little grin on his face. It was one that could be easily overlooked by anyone not paying really close attention to the situation but it was most definitely there. "What are you up to, John Henderson?" she asked, slipping around Vincent for a few seconds to try and catch the last part of the text message but the boy simply shifted the screen out of view.

"You'll find out," he grinned, glancing towards their Grandmother who was standing at the gateway to the house looking like a Matriarch who was not best pleased with this situation and was about to make it even more fouler than it could be, "It'll shut her up for a few precious moments, I can say that much."

Phoebe was about to press the matter when a sharp cough escaped Christina who glared at them through her beady black eyes. "What do you think you are doing, leaving the likes of me waiting on the doorstep like a pauper?" No one had the faintest idea as to why the woman talked like she was from the Victorian Era but there were just some things that were never asked. "I have been waiting here for fifteen minutes and I informed you that I would be here at precisely two o'clock sharp!"

Strangely it was the very well-bred Penny who broke the silence. "I don't see what the big problem is Mrs Christina. By my reckoning it is only just gone half past one and when me and Scott drove by here around twenty minutes ago there was no taxi or car in the drive, so unless your watch is running fast there has been no ill will played on you in the slightest."

Before the wrath could be thrown upon the blessed girl, Lucy cut in. "Vincent's plane was delayed, Christina, that is why we are running late and I agree with Penny that your clock is certainly running fast as it is only just a little after half past one."

"That is no excuse!" the woman snapped, banging her black stick to the ground. It would be conceivable to think that the old woman had actually bothered to dress up for Halloween as she was in a full black dress with a very grey looking lace collar and her white hair pulled up into a sharp bun. The stick and the unfortunate sight of a very battered looking over-night bag gave the impression that she was pretending to be some scary governess who would come into the house and murder all the children in their sleep. In fact it was pretty probable that she would given half the chance and the ability to get away with it. A horrible thought but Grandmother Christina gave off that impression all the time and it had led, indirectly, to the subconscious hiding of anything that potentially could maim, wound or kill. Of course, she wasn't dressed for Halloween in the slightest either. That was just the way she always dressed and the sour look on her face told everyone that life was not going to be easy.

Phoebe was beginning to dread the fact that she would have to explain where she was going tonight, there would be hell fire to pay that much was certain. Though before anyone could even suggest that they all go inside for a nice cup of tea and a chat, whilst trying to find a vile of arsenic to put into the correct cup, there came the sound of running feet and a voice calling, "Hey! Phoebe!"

Turning around, the girl's heart nearly burst into two separate emotions. Her newly appointed boyfriend was running up the street towards them, back pack slung artfully over his white t-shirt which was tucked into his black trousers. He had made an effort with his hair, slicking it back and putting it into a nice looking pony tail and was carrying a couple of expensive looking shopping bags. "Tony?" she asked, in a voice half filled with joy and half with horror. "What are you doing here? You're not supposed to pick me up till five!"

Coming to a stop, Tony grinned cheekily at the girl. "Well I thought I would come and surprise you. Boyfriends are allowed to do that, aren't they?"

"What?" The venom in the tone was enough to make Phoebe close her eyes and hang her head, whilst the boy looked innocently up at the old woman with a slight raising of his eyebrow – a clear sign he had been caught slightly off guard by the comment. "I'm her boyfriend, what's the matter with that?"

Grandmother Christina stormed forward, almost snarling in anger only to be stopped by a fearsome looking John and Scott who had almost formed an honour guard over the pair. "Leave her alone, Granny," John said, his voice low and dangerous, "she's allowed to pick who she likes and you're not going to hurt her for it."

"Most definitely not!" Tony said, pulling Phoebe close and wondering just what the hell he had walked into. "No one hurts my girl, even if they are related."

"Get out of my way, boy," the old woman snarled, "before I strike you a hundred times for your vile behaviour!"

No one was ever quite sure what happened next, a comment came from somewhere that infuriated the old woman into a blazing anger which caused her to lash out at John though he had not made the comment. Scott and Vincent were immediately trying to stop her hitting the boy anymore, Lucy was pulling Alan out of harm's way and Tony was trying to pull John out of the fray despite the fact that the old woman managed to get three more strikes on the male twin and one just nicked Tony's ear.

Phoebe tried to plead with the insane woman, but was caught by the stick which was swung around in an arch in an attempt to get Scott and Vincent so that the old woman's malice and anger could be directed at Lucy who was desperately trying to pull her boys back whilst keeping herself safe. The very most tip of the stick was covered in a simple metal stub which had worn away but was at just the right angle to scrape along the skin of the girl's cheek and draw blood.

Whilst it didn't hold that much strength, in comparison to what the woman could do in some given circumstances, it had been enough to knock Phoebe sideways and staggering. She barely had time to register the fact that she was close to the road when she suddenly found herself in the protective embrace of a man that she had not been held in for a very long time. "Mother!" the military commander snapped out, his green eyes almost glowing with disbelief about what was going on here, "what do you think you are doing to my family!"

Jeffery Henderson's voice was like that of a drill sergeant, cold and straight to the point but mixed with the years upon years of training as a loving father, gentle husband and proud defiant who wouldn't give in to anyone so easily. He towered over his mother by a good several foot and glared down at her from this impressive height without so much as a glimmer of flinching under the other's gaze.

Phoebe didn't want to believe it for one second that her father was back, holding onto her protectively but she was so thankful that tears began to fall down her face as she dug herself deep into his protective aura and prayed that this whole situation would blow over very soon.

Chapter 10

Daddy

Sitting in the room that was exclusively used for adults, Lucy and Jeff sat on separate single sofas and stared at nothing for a while. It was strange, life was full of uncertainties right now and neither one wanted to speak a word. "When did you get out of the hospital?" Lucy asked quietly looking up at her husband with a very worried gaze and noting just how healthy he looked. Okay there were the slight sighs of mistreatment, that maybe he had been eating a fair few pork pies or something similar but nothing that a few good sessions at the gym would get rid of. He was still regally handsome, his black hair, cut short, though it failed to hide the peppering of white segments which were creeping through. His eyes were exactly how she remembered them, glistening green and so warmly inviting that all she wanted to do was pull him into the deepest hug that she could do and kiss him passionately. But there was something not right about this situation, something almost ghostly and unreal.

"John's boyfriend gave me a lift," Jeff managed to look just a little on the suitably embarrassed side and rubbed the back of his head in wonder for a moment or two, "we got caught out by the flight times and—"

"That's not what I meant," the nearly-frantic woman managed to get in, waving her hands back and forth as if they were on fire. "I mean, how did you get here? You... you... this makes no sense!"

Lucy had been highly surprised to see how her boys had acted as if there was nothing unusual in their dead father suddenly appearing to them and they were all so glad about it. Grandmother Christine had immediately ordered a taxi and gone off home in a strop which had improved everyone's mood drastically but Lucy still felt an eerie sort of presence around the other. It was like being in a maze of glass and mirrors, you could never quite tell where the next walk way was even though you could see it if you adjusted your way of seeing the world. She knew that Jeff was sitting across from her, she could feel every part of her being longing to take him into her arms and hold him there forever but the rational part of her mind was telling her that it couldn't be him sitting there.

Jeff smiled serenely at his wife, going through the same emotions in his heart but knowing something about this situation in his head. He wouldn't speak of that knowledge though because it would only upset the most beautiful woman in the world in front of him and that was the last thing he wanted. Watching the way she subconsciously ran her fingers back and forth across her knee out of nervousness, the way her blue eyes bore into his soul to try and strip him bare and reveal him to be nothing but some impostor who could fool everyone else but also the glimmer of hope that radiated out from her. Lucy wanted to believe that this was real, her hope had never flickered or died and that for the man who had often wished to see her again was enough. He knew that she despised lies but to speak the truth would be enough to undo the wonder of this world and right now he didn't want to do that. Jeff smiled, sighing a little bit and lowering his head. "You're right, I didn't get out of the hospital. Lucy, you know that and I know that as well." Gently he took her wandering hand, which had led to her being nicknamed 'kitten' when they were dating. "You know the old legends of All Hallows Eve, your mama used to tell them to you every year and you told them to our wonderful children to carry on the tradition."

Lucy swallowed. "You're… a spirit who has returned?" There was a hint of disbelief but it was only so mild that it would be easy to push to one side.

Jeff nodded. "Yes, I've been allowed to come and visit you all for one final time. Don't ask me how I wrangled it because I'll never figure out such a thing but just for one night I'm back here with you, the boys and Phoebe." There came the sound of happy barking from the rooms below. "Where I belong. Not forgetting the dogs of course but I think it would be very hard to—"

Before Jeff could finish his sentence, he found himself engulfed by Lucy who was unashamedly covering the man's face and lips in kisses which hadn't been delivered for an untold length of time. A part of Jeff died, knowing that he had willingly led this fine woman down the garden path but there were some things that could not be taken back to easily. He was once again seeing his beautiful wife, able to hold her and know that it was not some dream. Plus, he had held the daughter he had only seen briefly for a day and an hour, which was something that he never thought he would ever do.

Jeff had promised John that he would speak to Phoebe, but right now his attention was firmly on Lucy and it was quite clear that it was going to be on his wife for at least the next hour or so.

~

In the general room on the second floor of the house, all of the Henderson children were happily gathered to sit on the various chairs, bean bags and other odds and ends that were safe for sitting on. Of course there were three additions to the normal numbers in the room, chiefly being Tony who was fussing over the mark on Phoebe's cheek whilst Penny was dealing with the bruises that were forming on John's chest and legs. They were looking pretty nasty already and John hissed as some more deep heat cream was rubbed in delicately as possible. "Ow! Penny, that hurts!"

"I'm trying my best," Penny said with a slightly annoyed sigh but she fully understood the boy's pain. "If you would just keep a little more still then it wouldn't be so painful."

A soft gentle chuckle escaped the third addition to the room, as a nicely toned arm wrapped itself around John's torso. "You seriously expect the likes of him to remain calm in a situation like this? I have enough trouble trying to get him to hold still in the bedroom, believe me, honey." Terry's dry wit and humour had made him an instant hit with the rest of the family, plus the fact that he had been absolutely straight in sorting everything out. His tall appearance, athletic build and dazzling smile had definitely caused a stir amongst the children but they weren't worried about anything in the slightest. His dark mahogany-coloured skin contrasted nicely with John's pale milky colouring and made them appear to be at completely opposite ends of the scale.

"Way more information that I ever needed to know," Penny said with a grin, stepping back slightly whilst John tried to dig his boyfriend in the side. "Here, why don't you put this on him instead and save us all a big hassle?"

Scott chuckled, catching hold of Penny to pull her back into his lap. "Please, the last thing I need to hear is my little brother getting turned on. I'm having enough trouble with the terrible twosome over there secretly snogging when they think we're not looking."

Picking up a nearby cushion, he expertly threw it at Tony and Phoebe only to find that his sister was looking down at the floor, redder than any beetroot he had ever seen whilst the boy just caught the pillow with a laugh. "Yeah, like you never made out in front of your siblings, Scott. I could probably tell your lovely little lady a story or two which would shatter her illusions about you being the perfect gentleman."

"Can we not have the lovers' quarrels?" Vincent asked from his position of being sprawled on the largest cushions with Diesel resting on his head and Amberly spread out across the floor in front of him. Though the latter was eyeing Alan who had a big, brightly-coloured ball bouncing back and forth in his hands. "Or whatever it is these days? I seriously cannot be bothered to put up with it all."

"You're just jealous because yours is all the way in Japan and you won't see him for a few weeks because someone was an idiot and got himself so worked up that he got a cold," Phoebe teased, sticking her tongue out at Vincent before throwing the pillow at John and Terry to catch them off guard.

Alan, feeling slightly left out, flopped onto the one sibling who wasn't being hugged or kissed by anyone right now. Vincent groaned a little and rolled over to tackle-hug the boy. "I'm never going to go out with a girl! They're icky!"

Vincent rolled his eyes. "We're still going through that phase with him?" he asked before tickling the boy who was trying to wriggle out of his grasp. Sometimes being at home was way better than being on stage with seventy thousand girls all screaming your name out. He was highly thankful that his parents had been awesome enough to allow him to call Kirei despite the call cost being really high and talk over their situation. Really the call had lasted thirty seconds as all Vincent had said was that he accepted and the rest had been an incomprehensible mush of languages.

"Yup," everyone replied before giggling and settling down. There were still a few hours before they had to get ready and it was nice to just be able to enjoy each other's company for a short amount of time.

Mentally Tony did a head count and sighed, "Hmm, getting this many people in to shot is going to be fun."

"What?" asked Scott, turning his head towards him with a slight frown.

"They're going to take a family photo of us all in our Halloween costumes," filled in John, shifting a little to make his life easier. "A bit like Adams Family, just without the strange theme music."

Vincent turned to look at Phoebe. "Seriously?"

The girl nodded a little shyly. "Yes, we are. It's about high time that we had a full photo and what better excuse to have our costumes? Don't worry, Tony's good at creating stuff if you didn't bring anything."

"Ha, this is why I love the fact that I live with my ma," Terry cut in, his brash accent still slightly jolting but fun to hear none the less. The tall male carefully ensured that John was resting comfortably on some of the cushions before wandering over to one of the suitcases he had brought with him and flinging it open. "I know that Halloween's not as big as it is at home but I think I've got more than enough stuff in here to help us celebrate it."

The bag was filled with costumes, masks and decorations for the house and it wasn't long before the entire clan, with the exception of the dogs, were up and about the house somewhere decorating or else sorting everything out. Phoebe went with Tony and Terry to set up the summer house properly for the big event but paused on the stairwell as she spotted a note with her name written on it. "Meet me at five thirty in the adult's room upstairs, Daddy."

Carefully folding it, the girl hurried to find the others whilst slipping the note into her pocket. It would be easy to slip away with all the commotion going on and a thrill of excitement ran through her system. But she kept herself in check, knowing that they had many different things yet to do on this day.

Chapter 11

The Room at the Top of the Stairs

As the clock struck five thirty, Phoebe found it easy to slip away from her brothers and sister-in-law to be. They were still in the process of trying to work out how to wear the complicated series of costumes which Terry had brought over and clearly the argument was going to last a long while. Sometimes boys could genuinely be more argumentative than girls, it was something really funny to watch. Still the girl knew that she needed to be careful right now, this was technically forbidden territory and if her mother caught her on the stairs... she didn't want to think of the consequences. Pausing exactly on the half-way step, the furthest she had ever gone before, the pale skinned girl looked up the stairs and felt as if she were at the very precipice of a life changing decision. An involuntary shudder went through her system and sharply she turned, flinging her hand out towards something that she caught out of the corner of her eye.

There was nothing to see, just a gentle laughter which seemed to exist only in her head and the girl shook it viciously, "Stop it, Phoebe, you're scaring yourself over nothing. You're just going to talk with your... dad who's dead." Even to the worried figure on the stairs it sounded absolutely silly but there was nothing else for her to do. She had told John that if she had been given the chance then she would speak to her father once again and now it had presented itself, she didn't know how to react in the slightest. Part of her mind was dancing for joy, bouncing around like a child at Christmas and instinctively most of her subconscious took refuge there.

But there was another part of her, just a small little figure standing in the light that was shrouded in darkness. It seemed to Phoebe that her fears were masquerading as a little girl, lost in a big wide world and terrified of taking another step forward even though the path was littered with friendly glowing lights. It had been the exact same feeling she had so many months, years ago when her father had been rushed into hospital. Lucy had never really confided in her children what was wrong and only ever took them to see the apparently slumbering man on very rare occasions. Phoebe had only been to visit him twice, the second time not long after her first encounter with John but unfortunately there had been a quarantine situation and they had not been permitted to enter.

However the girl still remembered the first time she had gone into the hospital with her mother to see her father after the accident. She had been about eight or nine at the time and everything in her memory distorted itself. The corridors had been long, bare of anything nice to look out and there was such a stench about the place, the chemically clean smell which invaded her nostrils and brought back some instinctual nightmare that made her want to turn around and run all the way back to the car. Somehow she had managed to stay right beside her mother and enter the room where her father was sleeping.

Another shiver went through her system as she remembered the gaunt, thin looking man who had been strapped to the bed with what appeared to be a series of tubes. Blood dripped down from an IV pack suspended high above the bed in her innocent young eyes and there was a plastic tube sticking out of the man's face. His skin was taught and wrinkled, not the usual bright colours that it appeared to be and his long dark hair had been shaven off in preparation for some form of operation that they were going to carry out. The small girl had lasted around thirty seconds in the room before she let out a cry and ran away in desperation, still just too young to understand what she was witnessing yet fully aware of the consequences of those things. It had affected her greatly, to the point where Lucy had nearly taken her to a child psychologist in order to help her out.

However, thankfully the little girl came up with her own way of dealing with the situation. A game where her father was just off working in some distant country and would eventually return to them all. As she got older of course the pretend faded, understanding filtering into her subconscious so that it became just a subject that wasn't talked about. She understood the situation all too well and whilst she would always cling to the hope that one day he would come back to them all, her adult mind knew that Jeff Henderson would not be coming back. Even at the funeral she found it hard to let go of the hope that maybe, some day, some chance encounter or just one more wish would allow her to see the man she had missed for the past nine years just one more time.

Blinking, Phoebe placed her hand on the banister and forcibly pulled herself up the stairs with the knowledge that if she wasted this chance then she would never get the opportunity granted ever again. Even if she forgot everything afterwards, like she had done before, then a part of her would be at peace for the first time in a long while. Nearly jumping out of her skin when the door to the parent's sanctuary opened, Phoebe paused at the top of the stairs as her blue eyes met the emerald green ones which smiled happily upon seeing her. Though there was some uncertainty there too, a hidden fear that was equally received and shared by both persons.

A silence of questioning passed between the pair before suddenly Jeff smiled and chuckled. "Look at us, standing here like a pair of ninnies. Come on, sweetheart, we have lots to talk about in only a short time." Gently, he offered her his hand and the girl noticed the roughness of the countless years of work that he had done. She noted the darker shade of his skin, but knew instinctively that it was due to him working out in Africa and Australia a lot of late. She blinked, taking in his image and finding all the faults that were supposed to be there even though she should only see the beauty. But that was one of the many miracles about being a young woman, instead of seeing what another might see in the man she saw only her father and all the small things that made him what he was.

Without thinking as to why, or really caring to be completely truthful, the dancer flung herself upon the man and held him tight. She smelt the various oils and other chemical substances which he worked with, though they were much faded these days and could feel the old smoothness that used to gently carry her to sleep whenever scary dreams haunted her. She felt his strength, his protectiveness and the love he held for each member of the family. Vaguely she noted that he was also glistening slightly with sweat as well but shoved those thoughts straight into the biggest lockable chest that she could do in her head and ignored them. "It really is you," she managed to stammer out, feeling tears pricking at her eyes. "I mean… you really are you. Oh I don't know what I'm saying but I don't care! I've got you back, Daddy, and that's all I want right now."

"Hush," Jeff said lightly, rubbing his thumbs over the girl's eyes and wishing that he could somehow go back in time and correct whatever happened to make him lose his little girl. "Phoebe, don't forget that in this world I'm not here. I'm not quite the man who has the right to claim himself as your father but I wish I was."

Staring down at the girl, he saw why John had described her as an Angel. Like the ones that you got on top of the tree if you went to the right shops and bought a proper one. The girl was pale like her twin with such lovely blonde hair that she looked more like a doll than anyone else in the world. Her eyes shimmered brightly, so like Lucy's, and were so innocent and sweet that Jeff just wanted to be held in that gaze forever. He had promised to not get too attached but how could he possibly not do when it meant having to give up something as precious as a daughter?

"But you have memories, right?" Phoebe asked in a panic. "Like me and John! We remember things that can't have happened and then forget them."

Jeff nodded, running his fingers down the side of the girl's face. "Yes, Phoebe, I have those memories. I remember taking you to the park when you lost your favourite dolly, I remember watching every last one of your dance recitals and the amount of times I've argued with you about going over to Japan to dance on your brothers show and use his contacts I've lost track of." It was a strange situation but Jeff didn't mind in the slightest. They were precious and gentle memories, the type that could be clung to in the middle of the night but they weren't what he wanted to talk about right now. "But all of that is just what's needed, Lucy… your mother, is under the impression that I'm a spirit who's returned because of it being All Hallows, you know what she's like for believing such things and I don't want her to think of it as anything else."

Phoebe tilted her head to the side, scrutinising him carefully. "You've told her that you've put a spell on me and the others so they won't question anything haven't you?"

Chuckling, Jeff nodded and pushed the girl away gently just so he could get an idea of her height. She was definitely smaller that John but that didn't matter. He had known instinctively that what he had to give the girl was going to be perfect. "You could say that, now I want you to do me a favour and dry your tears because your old man has a gift for you and he wants to see what you look like in it."

Frowning, the girl watched Jeff as he made his way over to the opposite side of the room in order to pull out a large cardboard box. Faintly she heard the sound of the shower running nearby and was able to work out where her mother was which caused a smile to creep across her face. "Now," Jeff's voice drew her attention back to him, "I don't want you to comment on the price or anything like that. I just want you to say if you like it or not."

Presenting the box to his daughter, Jeff watched with just a touch of nerves as the girl took it from him and placed it down on the nearest table. Gently she removed the lid and put aside the tissue paper which was added to keep everything nice and gentle looking. Phoebe's eyes widened as she stared down at the dress, which was a beautiful deep satin red similar to the colour of a dark rosé wine. Carefully she lifted it up and stared at it in wonder. It was a corset dress, with simple straps and elegant dark yellowy gold embroidery around the flared skirt which twirled back and forth. The top was laced with very fine silver thread and there was a tiny pearl in the centre.

It was exquisite beyond anything that she had seen before and even came with a handful of accessories. Phoebe stared at it in question before looking up towards Jeff. "But, how? This has been on display forever and no one can ever afford it!"

Jeff smiled. "You're daddy's a good businessman, plus I am sure that the girl who wears such a thing to any ball will certainly be one of the most charming queens. Now, before you say it, I know that red usually does not work on you but I managed to get John to try on a shirt the exact same colour and it worked on him, so it'll work on you just fine, sweetheart."

Staring down at the dress once again, remembering how many times she had just looked into the window of the fancy shop on the high street and wished that she could wear it herself, Phoebe once again found herself in her father's arms but this time it would be out of nothing more than love and respect for a man whom she would only know a few hours. Not that it mattered much of course, to spend a single moment with someone was often more worthwhile than spending an entire entity with them.

"Now, we best get ready for that photo otherwise we'll never get Miss Phoebe to the ball." Jeff smiled, trying to hide his own tears as he scuttled the girl off to get sorted out. He knew there was going to be a big stir over this but did he care? No, to have this was worth ten times anything else in the world right now. He had his family, his beautiful wife and a daughter whom he could spoil rotten. What more was a man to want in life?

Chapter 12

Photographic Arrangements

The hours had ticked by quietly but the entire household appeared to be in some form of great flurry of activity. It was barely just after six thirty and already there were the jovial sounds of laughter and the friendly argumentative shouting which always appeared to infect houses when large families were together. Well at least the ones who got on with one another on a more understanding basis rather than ending up in a big free for all bout on the floor. Though throughout the years such things had occurred more than once throughout the house but that was the sometimes tricky part of having four to five sons and a daughter all trying to live together. Some day's it worked absolutely fine and other days it was nothing short of divine intervention that stopped them all from grabbing the kitchen knives and killing each other.

Lucy smiled as she sat in the summer house, waiting for her children to stop arguing about who looked better in what and actually get to the house before it was too dark to do anything. However Tony had wisely and thankfully thought ahead and had enlisted the help of his friend Andrew who had a selection of professional lights and colour boards for capturing the right mood. It was clear which one was the more professional photographer but as Andrew explained he was going onto a degree the following September so most of this was just the basic stuff he had been able to get hold of in order to play around with over the summer. "I think that should just about do it," Andrew said, checking the image of Lucy through the view finder as it would be him who would be taking the photo so that Tony didn't have to run back and forth like a crazy man in order to get everything done. "Of course, I might have to reset depending on what people are wearing but I'm sure it'll be fine."

After it had been revealed that the general clothes collection which Terry had brought across from the states had all revolved around the theme of aristocratic vampires – though he refused to actually say what fiction they were based off – there had been some grumblings but everyone had agreed that at least they would all look the part. John didn't appear overly happy about the situation and mother and son had confided in the fact that it meant he would be wearing a suit which was usually reserved for the live action role play games which he and Terry were involved in. Just in those particular games, John was Terry's factotum who was also a blood bank at the same time. Lucy didn't quite understand the whole concept or why John would be so upset about such a thing but passed it off as being something that she would rather not learn about.

"Yeah? That's a good thing to know, I would hate to have to reset everything three times because of that, it would take forever and a day to do," Tony said, leaning back a little and sighing.

Lucy eyed him critically. "Shouldn't you be getting changed? I dread to think what the photo would look like if you were in nothing but those jeans and a T-shirt."

Chuckling loudly, Andrew grinned and winked. "Oh, don't worry, he's just concerned about having to actually preen himself for once. He'll get changed, Mrs Henderson, and if he doesn't I'll post the most embarrassing image up of him on the internet and there's no way he'll ever live it down."

For a while there was only general banter between the small groups until the rest of the family started to arrive. Some felt rather odd to be in this sort of situation whilst others were enjoying the chance to flaunt their new fashions with a bit more glee than what they were really supposed to do. Of course everyone was initially interested in what Lucy was wearing as no one had seen the dark blonde-haired woman leave the house. She was dressed in a long flowing ivory white dress which was covered in dark purple branches with light red roses on the ends. A medieval style cloak in a deep blue with green lining was held over her shoulders by a white cord and her hair was pulled up into a high pony tail with a selection of fake flowers carved into it. There was a staff lying around but Lucy couldn't be bothered with it all the time as she was having enough troubles placing the false teeth in the right place.

Her husband looked almost the exact opposite of her white and innocent vampire, he was clad in rich reds and dark blacks of a full tuxedo suit complete with waistcoat and billowing black cape with the blue inner lining contrasting nicely to everything. His hair, though thinning and short, had been gelled up to have a slight curl at the front and just the hint of spikes around the back and sides. Having raided the old costume box which the Henderson's constantly kept on forgetting about, Jeff had added a few silver accessories to his appearance, namely involving a pocket watch and a pair of stunning white gloves. To his bride he gave a dazzling fake diamond necklace and matching bracelet. He was going to give her a tiara to go with it but the general consensus was that it didn't quite go with the overall flow.

Scott and Penny were next and it was very hard to recognise them at first. For once Penny had let her strawberry-blonde hair down and it shimmered in a long waterfall effect that fanned out around her back. She was dressed simply in an old fashioned debutants dress which had been artfully ripped and torn to make it appear that she had been snatched away from some dazzling event by the impressive vampire and was completely in his thrall. She even had two fake bite marks dawn in with makeup on her neck to match the situation. Scott looked ever the part as he always did, dressed in black trousers with a white shirt, dazzling gold buttons and a dark blue sash around his middle. His hair was also gelled up, though into a much more appropriate style and a bit of dark eyeliner had been applied to give him a much more severe looking appearance. He had forgone on the lipstick though, refusing to have any on, not even to create the illusion that he had just drunk from his future wife.

Pretending to be highly annoyed but clearly enjoying the fact that he was receiving a lot more attention from Terry than anyone else had perceived at this point in time, John looked completely unlike himself with a pair of brown trousers, much plainer white shirt and a jacket which looked as though it had been stolen wholesale from number 221B Baker Street. His blond hair was smothered lovingly down by Terry, and he even consented to wearing the fake glasses with the gold rims. They looked surprisingly good on him and for an added little joke he was carrying an old looking copy of one of the most famous vampire books in the history of literature. Not that this fact stopped Terry from tormenting the poor boy in his vampire garb which clearly had some effect on the other though he was trying to deny it completely. Terry was dressed in an elegant looking shirt with dramatic flowing over coat and wore only sandals on his feet but somehow they fitted in with his eccentric character. He wore gold buttons, had his hair twisted into a series of winding knots and was perfectly able to wrap himself around John in such ways that it was next to impossible to imagine that the other had any chance of escaping.

In his own way, Vincent was glad to be able to get into the swing of things as most of his photo shoots were there to simply please the girls and generally he had no control over them. If it was him and his band mates just larking about then it was pretty much free for all but most of the time it was all arranged in advance and there was no chance of being allowed to do what he liked. Since he had been given pretty much free reign, he had opted to do the 'sexy' look and wore an open buttoned shirt with dark purple trousers and a heavy-looking manacle set which had been broken off at the chains on his wrists and neck though the manacles remained in place. They had also come from a raid on the costume box where there had possibly been the chance of an exploding collar but he opted out of wearing such a thing. A few drops of fake blood completed his look, and all of the brothers and boyfriends were annoyed by the fact that he barely needed to do anything else to have the look down which would threaten their chances. Not that it would happen of course, it was just all part of the game.

Alan looked like a young Victorian school boy with his cap twisted at a strange angle and big black circles around his eyes. He had wanted a suit but unfortunately there was nothing that was really his size until the cap had flopped out. It was a very distinguished looking uniform, clearly meant for someone who attended a very important looking school and somehow the naughty eight-year-old whose only fondness in life revolved around giant robots battling turned out to be quite the actor and seemed to know exactly where he needed to place himself. Andrew smiled and chuckled, shaking his head as Tony emerged wearing a very dashing looking suit complete with top hat, cane and scarf though as he had said earlier it was more to do with the fact that he was going to a ball later on with Phoebe, "Well you won't need to worry about not fitting in, you're going to match perfectly with this lot."

"Where's Phoebe?" asked Alan, getting a bit huffy because Diesel was trying to nick off with his hat despite the fact that the poor thing had been wrangled into a bow tie and mini top hat not ten minutes ago.

Lucy looked around, doing a headcount. "Actually, you're right, I haven't seen her in a long while."

Sighing lightly, Tony shook his head in amazement as he fixed some of the complicated make-up on his face. It was to make him appear more of an zombie gentleman, the type who wandered into posh balls to snatch young maidens away to the dark underworld, but more of the type that were grey in skin tone and seemed sunken in humans that were turning into skeletons,

"She's probably just having a nightmare with her hair, it's usually the reason that she run's late for anything."

"Actually it's trying to walk in high heels across that expanse of garden," Phoebe's voice drifted in from the doorway where she stood framed in her brand new red dress. She looked stunning, like a ghost who could only wander the earth once a year in order to seek out the hand of the man who had told her to wait. Part of her hair was neatly brushed back and tied into a thin braid whilst the rest ran roughly down past her shoulders in a series of crazy riverettes. The red ball gown which Jeff had gotten her was just as stunning as the father believed it to be and just a few touches of makeup had extended the girl's natural paleness and turned it into a glorious beauty. There was an immediate fuss of course, normally the girl never appeared in anything that didn't cover her pale skin and draw attention to herself. Tony smiled and placed a kiss on her lips in the midst of all the commotion. "I believe the ghost queen has arrived."

"Can we get on with this photo, ladies and gents?" Andrew asked with a big grin on his features. "Not meaning to be rude or anything but if we don't take it then the bell of the ball will definitely be running late."

The photos were taken, a total of fifteen in all with the family arranged in different positions just so that they would have at least a choice once the pictures were correctly developed. Of course only three of the family count knew that tomorrow not all of them would be waking up in the same house as before with all the same family members present but for that moment it was a surprising lovely revelation just to be able to share in a moment of family bliss.

Chapter 13

The Wish

Carefully walking downstairs, which she wasn't quite used to, Phoebe stretched and touched the crossbeam with her fingers for good luck. It was a habit which Jennifer, Tony's mother, had told her when she had first visited the house so many years ago and it was something that she kept up with a pride. A smile crossed her features as she stared around the simple little home and was glad that she wasn't hampered by those lovely high heels that she had been wearing throughout all of last night. The ball had been and gone, almost as if it were in some form of dream but that hardly bothered the girl. It had been a glorious affair of colours, wild dancing and some rather surprising costumes and couples wandering around. She had enjoyed herself greatly before returning home with Tony as it was an easier option than trying to get to the other side of town at three in the morning when they only had three pounds left between them to spend.

Thankfully, Lucy had had the foresight to send an overnight bag across to Tony's house which meant no embarrassing situations except the ones that they created for themselves but with Jennifer already out of the door to head to work things like that wouldn't be covered until at least midday. Walking through the stone floored kitchen, almost cursing the fact that she had no slippers on her feet, the girl headed for the only source of noise in the house. It came from a little work station which had been set up as a dark room and photo development lab and it was clear that Tony and Andrew were in their element.

Knocking quietly on the door, the girl smiled as her boyfriend opened it a fraction to see who it was and then allowed her access. "Morning. Did you sleep all right?"

"When I got some sleep, yes I did thank you," Phoebe chuckled, glad when the other pulled her into a hug and pressed a kiss against her lips.

"Put her down," Andrew said in mock annoyance. "The last thing I need is for your kissing germs to be over all of these prints."

Rolling his dark eyes skywards, Tony returned to his task at hand whilst Phoebe made her way carefully around the room on the pretext of trying to find a chair. It was a perfectly valid excuse which would allow her to get a good look at the pictures which were already developed and drying off. Normally these rooms needed a red light to be glaring around them all of the time but the formula they were using was designed to deliberately age the produced images so it wasn't that big of a problem. She smiled at the familiar ones of herself in some of the dresses that Tony had designed and found the most recent addition of her own hand made dress with the pumpkins had come out in a very lovely looking style.

However she blinked upon finding that the next set of pictures contained herself and a figure whom at first she did not recognise. Frowning, the girl tried to remember back to the pictures that were being taken prior to the ball and nearly panicked for a second when she didn't remember a thing. Staring at the boy, her blue eyes blinked slowly and a thought, small and easy to ignore whispered, "Remember the tales of Hallows Eve, that's what you do my dear sister."

Reaching her fingers forward as if to touch the picture, Phoebe stopped upon remembering the fact of what could happen if done before everything was set firmly in the right place. Turning back to Tony and Andrew, she smiled, "Do either of you remember who the boy is in these pictures?"

Andrew looked up from his work, casting a quick glance over his shoulder. "We were hoping that you could fill us in actually. It gave us both a real fright to see him standing there."

"Yeah," Tony agreed though he didn't sound quite into the conversation as he normally would be, "but not as big a fright as these ones. I have no clue as to when they were taken or what's going on in them either."

Drawing herself closer to the trays, where the pictures were currently dripping their special mixture into, Phoebe stared at the full photograph of her family in one of the many poses which they had arranged themselves into. She smiled at the classic image of the head of the household with all of his children spread about his feet and wondered at the long image of them all rising up out of furniture as if they had been asleep forever. However her favourite one featured herself seated on the wooden high back chair with the same boy from the other picture next to her. Unlike the other family photos, his costume had changed to a matching red shirt to her dress and black trousers. Their eyes were closed and their hands clasped together with trails of blood running down their necks.

Tony and Terry stood either side of them, matching their partners exactly whilst in the background the rest of the family waited to welcome them to the interior of a dark looking mansion. The effect was pretty good, considering it was just the summer house in her garden and the chair had been manhandled out into the night sky. Phoebe understood the deeper meaning of the piece though, why she and the boy had requested to do such a strange image. It was simple; they were together in an eternal slumber which could only be crossed at certain times by a method that could not be seen in this image. "Remember the tales of All Hallows Eve? When the dead can walk amongst the living, taking on their roles as if nothing had ever happened to them?" Tony said slowly.

It was Andrew who rallied first. "You mean this is something to do with the stuff your mum goes on about? About souls getting to come back from the dead?"

Phoebe nodded. "It's the only explanation I can think of. It's slightly creepy but that's what I think it is. Of course it could be that Mum was having a party for some of her friends last night and we got them to join in on the photo."

"Suppose so," Tony sighed. "It's not like me to forget something like that though."

"You were drinking a lot last night, my dear," the girl laughed before squealing when the boy tickled her viciously in return for such a comment. In the end they all agreed that it was just a bunch of extra people from the party who had been asked to join in and since apparently Tony had hired a male model that looked incredibly similar to Phoebe, they had managed to get him involved as well.

Carefully wrapping up her copies to take home later that morning, Phoebe paused at the twin picture again and smiled at it fondly. She had asked for far more copies than she normally would but both boys were happy to provide them. "I don't remember your name but I know who you are and where you'll want to find these photos. I hope one day that we'll be able to meet again, even if it is only for a brief time."

Placing the picture carefully back into its protective covering, the dancer went to the home that she always had known and loved. She spent the day talking to her mother about the ball, trying to appease inquisitive brothers who wanted to know far more than they were ever going to get the chance to know and playing with the dogs who were more hyperactive than normal. In comparison to the last few days it felt more normal, more gentle and serene but she couldn't quite equate as to why. Lucy had adored the pictures and fully agreed with her about the rumours of Hallows Eve. They made arrangements to get proper picture frames, as well as additional copies for the others as well. Vincent was particularly keen because he had been allowed to his own photo which would definitely have the internet abuzz once he got back into the flow of things but he wanted more than ever to get Kirei into his arms first.

Phoebe told no one of the extra set of prints which she had requested and that night, just as the clouds cleared away, the girl carefully slipped out of her bedroom to the other door. Normally this one was kept locked and not used by anyone though no one could honestly remember why. Finding the key had proved to be no problems in the slightest and as she entered, a shudder went through Phoebe's body. The room was surprisingly clean but extremely simple, set out in a standard layout that did not match her own. Not that she had expected it to but it was still a slight shock. There was a bed, the size for a child just coming out of the crib phase and it was covered in rockets and space symbols. There was a wardrobe which was left for the time being and a box of toys which had never been played with.

All of these were ignored by the girl who approached an old looking desk which had a large drawer and plenty of cubby holes for pens, pencils, books and other associated things. Carefully she opened the drawer, glad that the hinges gave off no sounds and placed the package into the space before closing it once again. Then, just to make sure, the young woman carefully scratched the initials 'JH+PH' on the surface with a nail. She wasn't sure as to what significance it would have but some part of her mind was convinced that it would do the job. Satisfied, Phoebe was about to return to her own room and go to sleep when instead she wandered over to the window instead.

Standing there, looking out over the window, she was faintly aware of another presence in the room approaching her. Without looking she knew that the other was soon standing right next to her, hand resting lightly on top of hers as if he were afraid that it would sink through. Phoebe didn't turn, instinctively knowing that she must not do such a thing and instead stared out at the stars. After what felt like an eternity of waiting, a star glistened more brightly for a few seconds and then disappeared off at tremendous speeds to another part of the galaxy. Phoebe smiled. "I wish that someday I may be able to see you again."

There was no response of course and a shiver went through Phoebe's body once again. Turning she headed back out of the room, carefully closing the door and locking it. She would have to return the key tomorrow morning but that was an easy enough job. Returning to her own warm bed, Phoebe lightly closed her eyes after a few moments of watching the strange gold and green lights dance around her room from the strange night light that had proved itself time and again to be a calming stimulus for the girl.

When the light switched itself off not a few minutes later, a softer white blue light streamed across the slumbering figures face as the cat like being gently ran his fingers through her hair. He smiled before placing a departing kiss on her forehead. "Wish granted… for another day." Raising the creature smiled again, before turning to the window and disappearing out into the night air where immediately he dissolved into a thousand tiny glowing sparkles that rose into the distant dark sky and were soon lost to the dark abyss of the vastness of the night.